Faceless Crime
Miami Syndicate

BY

TOMMY HERRERA

DEDICATION

I dedicate this book to my two sons, Mason and Alex. As a reminder that nothing is impossible when you focus, make small sacrifices and always stay on course.

ABOUT THE AUTHOR

Growing up on the streets of Chicago to the shores of Miami, my journey is a testament to resilience and the trans-formative power of fatherhood. Despite the challenges of leaving formal education early, I discovered profound lessons in the joys and responsibilities of raising two remarkable sons. My narrative is not just a personal chronicle but a tribute to the legacy of parental wisdom passed down from my late mother. Her guiding voice remains a beacon, illuminating my path and shaping the values I will instill in my boys. My story is a vivid illustration that life's richest education often comes from experiences and relationships, not just classrooms.

CONTENTS

Chapter 1

THE RISE OF GABRIEL CORTEZ

The city lights of Chicago flickered in the distance as the Cortez family made their way through the bustling streets. They were starting a new chapter in their lives, leaving behind the familiar comforts of the communist island of Cuba for the unknown challenges of the city, notorious for its corrupt politicians and gangsters. Joaquin's mind raced with a mixture of excitement and trepidation.

Justina, a 28-year-old Latina with dark hair and a short build, gripped the hand of Joaquin, her 30-year-old husband with a thick mustache and full beard, tightly. Her pulse quickened with a mixture of excitement and trepidation. Their two children, six-year-old Gabriel and four-year-old Elena, gazed out the window, wide-eyed at the towering skyscrapers and neon signs that seemed to stretch on forever.

"Are you sure about this, Joaquin?" Justina asked, searching her husband's face for any hint of doubt.

Joaquin Cortez had heard the stories, the legends of men who had risen from humble beginnings to become powerful players in the city's underworld. It was a world that fascinated him, a world where the rules were different, where strength and cunning were the keys to success. He had always been a survivor. He knew how to hustle, how to take care of himself. But the stories of Chicago's underworld, the way they commanded respect and wielded influence, stirred something deep inside him.

Settling into a predominantly white neighborhood in the Uptown area of Chicago in the 1970s, the Cortez family quickly discovered that acceptance was not readily extended to Hispanics like them. Discrimination and hostility haunted their daily lives, casting a dark shadow over their aspirations for a fresh start. For Gabriel, the harsh reality of his new surroundings fostered a sense of defiance, a determination to carve out his place in this unwelcoming world.

But Joaquin Cortez, Gabriel's father, knew that the path he was considering was a dangerous one, fraught with risk and temptation. He had seen what the lure of the streets could do to a person, how it could consume them, destroy them. Still, the allure was undeniable, the promise of wealth, power, and respect too tempting to ignore.

As Gabriel became more acquainted with his neighborhood, he witnessed the raw violence that simmered beneath the surface. Gang fights erupted with alarming frequency, some unfolding just steps away from his apartment building. The allure of the Latino gangs grew stronger, drawing him into their midst as a means of protection in this hostile environment at a young age.

Those formative years shaped him in ways he's still trying to understand. The violence he witnessed and the choices he made have left scars, both physical and emotional. But even now, he can't help but feel a sense of loyalty to the gang that once offered him protection and a sense of purpose, however twisted that may have been.

The violence was a constant backdrop to his daily life as a teenager growing up in the North-side of Chicago in the Uptown neighborhood. The sound of gunshots would echo through the streets, sending everyone scrambling for cover. Gabriel knew he needed to find a way to survive in this world.

Gabriel became entangled in the dangerous web of gang life and petty crimes became the norm, leading to his eventual arrest for disorderly conduct, possession of drugs, and other criminal activities. The irresistible lure to fit in and find a sense of belonging set Gabriel on a hazardous path. Embracing substances like marijuana, cocaine, and the prevailing drug of the era, became his initiation into the gritty street culture.

At 17, Gabriel found himself caught in a dangerous spiral. With each passing day, he became increasingly entangled in the gritty realities of gang life. Petty crimes and gang activity soon became the norm for him.

One day, his father's shady associates took notice of Gabriel's cunning street smarts. They approached him, sensing an opportunity. A low-level dealer sidled up to Gabriel, offering him a chance to make easy money. "Just keep quiet about what I'm offering you," the man whispered.

Swayed by the prospect of cash, Gabriel agreed. Soon, he was selling drugs to the older ç in the neighborhood.

As his business grew he was still a minor, unable to get into the local clubs, he would sit outside in the parking lot, peddling his wares to the partying crowds.

The money was good, and it gave Gabriel a sense of power and control he'd never known. But as he sank deeper into the criminal underworld, he couldn't shake the feeling that he was losing a part of himself. The thrill of easy cash was gradually being replaced by a creeping anxiety.

The repercussions of Gabriel's choices were profound,

as he slowly succumbed to the seduction of power and the temptation of fast, illicit gains, which only served to obscure the boundaries between his identity and the captivating allure of that tumultuous lifestyle.

As his involvement deepened, Gabriel's hunger for control and wealth intensified. He discovered a knack for making money and exploiting the opportunities presented by the streets. The drug trade became his new canvas, where he could paint a portrait of danger and profit. With each transaction, Gabriel felt a surge of adrenaline, the intoxicating thrill of living life on the edge. He had become a willing participant in the dark underbelly of Chicago's criminal underworld.

Gabriel and his family began to observe the escalating scrutiny and investigation into his activities within the neighborhood. The police persistently harassed him, routinely pulling him over and conducting thorough searches of his vehicle, hunting for weapons and drugs. With the constant pressure, it became apparent that Gabriel's inevitable incarceration loomed on the horizon, arriving sooner than anticipated.

Unknown to Gabriel, his father, Joaquin, and uncle were involved in a drug trafficking operation in Chicago. They were part of an organized crime ring that was bringing large quantities of narcotics into the city.

Gabriel was involved in the street lifestyle and criminal

activities and had been arrested a couple of times for the sale of narcotics. He was starting to draw unwanted attention and heat toward the entire operation. The authorities were getting dangerously close to uncovering the full scope of the family's illicit enterprise.

Realizing the increasing risk, Joaquin Cortez decided to uproot the family and move them all to Miami. He hoped that by removing them from Chicago, they could avoid any further police investigation or crackdown that could expose their family's deep ties to the drug trade.

Gabriel Cortez was kept in the dark about the real reasons behind the sudden move. As far as he knew, it was just another one of his father's impulsive decisions, not realizing the gravity of the situation they were fleeing.

Little did Gabriel suspect that his actions on the streets were inadvertently jeopardizing Joaquin Cortez and his uncle's criminal empire.

The family's relocation to Miami was a desperate attempt to outrun the consequences of their shady business dealings back in Chicago.

As they settled into their new home, an uneasy tension hung in the air, with Joaquin Cortez and his brother constantly on edge, slowly letting Gabriel Cortez into the inner circle of the organization.

The scorching Miami sun beat down on the city, its rays

searing the concrete and illuminating the vibrant colors of the sprawling landscape. Gabriel Cortez stood at the heart of it all, his eyes hidden behind a pair of designer sunglasses as he surveyed the bustling streets teeming with life. He could feel the energy pulsating through the air, a magnetic force that drew him in, promising untold possibilities.

Now in his 20s, Gabriel had already learned the hard lessons of street life. Joaquin Cortez and his associates had been grooming Gabriel for years, showing him the ropes of how to survive and thrive in their world of shady deals and shadowy alliances.

"Stay out of sight, never brag," Gabriel's father would tell him. "Let others take the fame and glory, while you pull the strings from behind the scenes. That's how you weather any storm."

Gabriel took his father's advice to heart. From a young age, he learned the art of manipulation, studying the motivations and weaknesses of those around him. While others sought the spotlight, Gabriel preferred to operate behind closed doors, exerting his influence through carefully placed suggestions and calculated moves.

As Gabriel grew older, he became a master at the game. He knew how to play people against each other, sow seeds of distrust, and always keep his involvement hidden. His father was impressed, seeing the ruthless pragmatism in his son that had served them all so well.

"You're a natural, boy," Joaquin would say with a proud grin. "With your head on your shoulders and your mouth shut, you'll outlast all of us. No one will ever see you coming."

And that was exactly how Gabriel liked it. Behind the scenes, pulling the strings that was where he thrived. The fame and glory meant nothing to him. Survival was the only thing that mattered.

Surprisingly, time passed, and there was no one above the law. Joaquin Cortez and his associates were secretly under harsh investigation for drug trafficking. The hammer came down, and Joaquin Cortez and the others were indicted and sentenced to 30 years in federal prison. Just like that, Gabriel's world came crashing down around him. He was now a solo soldier, forced to fend for himself in an unforgiving world.

As he observed the glamorous façade and the relentless pursuit of pleasure that defined Miami, Gabriel couldn't help but be captivated by the juxtaposition of light and darkness. Beyond the shimmering high-rises and extravagant beachfront properties of Miami Beach, he knew the obscure corners held secrets and dangers that few would dare to explore. It was within those hidden corners that he had thrived, embracing the chaos and unpredictability of the streets.

A sly smile played on Gabriel's lips as he contemplated

the shift from his former Chicago battleground to Miami's allure. His mind raced with thoughts of opportunity and ambition, knowing that he could carve out a new empire in this city. But he understood that it wouldn't be an easy task. Miami was a different beast altogether, where power and control were coveted by many yet attained by only a select few.

Miami was an open invitation to rewrite his legacy, a chance to rise above his previous accomplishments and establish himself as a force to be reckoned with. His thoughts were a torrent of calculated ambition, forming a strategy to navigate the intricate power dynamics within his family and the city itself.

"Miami," he whispered to himself, his voice a low murmur amidst the cacophony of the city. "A playground where fortunes are made and broken, where the line between friend and foe blurs into oblivion. It's time to leave my mark on this canvas of contradictions."

Gabriel's eyes flickered with determination as he embraced the heat and chaos that awaited him. He knew that Miami would test, challenge, and perhaps even break him. But deep down, he relished the opportunity, for it was within the crucible of this vibrant city that his true power would be forged.

While most of his former comrades found themselves behind bars for drug-related offenses, Gabriel remained a lone wolf, navigating the treacherous underworld with a hunger for more.

In the wake of his family and their associates' incarceration, Gabriel was trapped in an oppressive sense of stagnation. The walls of his modest apartment felt like a prison, each passing day fueling his yearning for new opportunities, another chance to amass wealth and influence. He longed to escape the suffocating grip of his past and forge a brighter future. During this pivotal moment, when the hot Miami sun bathed his room in a golden haze, an unexpected contact reached out to him.

Michael Cruz cast an imposing figure as he stalked the mean streets of Miami's criminal underbelly. Tall and rippling with muscle, the 28yearold Latino was a force to be reckoned with. His thinning hair was offset by a thick, scruffy beard that only added to his gruff, intimidating appearance.

Despite his young age, Michael had already carved out a reputation as one of Miami's most ruthless players. Always casually dressed in simple jeans and polo shirts, he commanded respect and instilled fear wherever he went. Those who crossed him quickly learned the hard way that he was not a man to be trifled with.

Gabriel, a sharp-dressed man in his early 30s of average build, approached this enigmatic character with caution. His mind raced, weighing the risks and rewards of engaging with someone of such a notorious reputation. Despite his reservations, Gabriel couldn't help but be intrigued by Michael's proposition laid out before him – a new avenue to explore that seemed to transcend all his previous ventures in the world of crime.

They met at a sidewalk restaurant in South Beach, clinking glasses and hushed conversations creating a cloak of anonymity around them. The figure leaned in, barely audible above the background noise, and spoke in hushed tones about the alluring world of white-collar crime. He painted a vivid picture of money flowing like a river; the risks seemed minimal compared to the constant threat of law enforcement and the dangerous underworld of drugs.

"The drug game is saturated, my friend," the shadowy figure whispered, his eyes glinting with mischief and calculation. "But there's another way that exploits a broken system. Gabriel, healthcare fraud is where the real fortuncs are made. The healthcare system is a mess, a maze of loopholes waiting to be exploited. It's a perfect setup? We remain faceless. I have individuals willing to open medical offices, and once we finish our scam, they will go back to Cuba. We stay here, untouched. No one knows who we are. It's a perfect setup."

Gabriel's brows furrowed as he considered the proposition. The allure of this new venture, where he could navigate the complexities of bureaucracy instead of the treacherous streets, enticed him. It promised a different kind of power that operated in the hidden realms of legality.

"So you can do this yourself?" Gabriel asked, his voice laced with skepticism.

Michael nodded. "Yes, Gabriel, but I need you to fund the project. I'm short on cash."

A heavy silence hung in the air as Gabriel weighed the risks. Leaving behind the world of drug deals for something more sophisticated held an undeniable appeal, but he knew better than to trust blindly.

"What's the catch?" he pressed, eyes narrowing.

Michael's gaze didn't waver. "No catch. Just a business opportunity that requires a little... creative navigation."

Gabriel's instincts screamed caution. He'd been in the game long enough to know that promises often concealed darker motives. The path Michael proposed might lead to wealth and influence, but at what cost?

He leaned back in his chair, the gears of his mind turning, weighing the risks against the potential rewards. His eyes darted around the sidewalk restaurant as he embraced the scene of exotic cars and beautiful women on Ocean Drive. The figure before him, seemingly unruffled by the weight of the conversation, let the silence hang in the air.

After what felt like an eternity, Gabriel leaned forward, his voice barely above a whisper. "Let's make it happen. I will fund the operation. This is the birth of the PMC—Product Manipulation Crew."

Gabriel's eyes burned with intensity as he laid out the ground rules. "Let's start making things clear from the start to avoid any problems later." He paused, his look piercing. "As I said, I will fund the project. But I want to stay behind the scenes. You talk to whoever you need to and make things happen. I will have your back no matter what."

"I don't wanna meet anyone, especially talk to anyone if I don't have to. And when you call me, never use a real name—always an alias."

"Let me give you this address so when we start making money, you can rent an apartment on Brick-ell Drive in Miami."

"I don't understand, Gabriel. Why do I need an apartment just to meet?" Michael questioned as he studied the address scribbled on the notepad.

Gabriel leaned back in his chair with a smile on his face. "I have a place there. Brick-ell Drive, right in the heart of Miami. High-rises, fancy shops, and a nightlife that never sleeps. It's the perfect cover."

"But the expense—"

"It's necessary," Gabriel cut him off. "We can't risk meeting in the open anymore. Too many eyes, too many ears. This way, once we're inside those walls, no one knows what happens."

Michael considered Gabriel's words. He couldn't deny the logic, as much as he disliked the idea of an unnecessary expense.

"All right, fine. I'll make the arrangements," Michael agreed. "But you'd better have a good reason for all this cloak and dagger."

"Michael, do you believe in your project that we will make a lot of money? Then trust me, my friend. You'll see soon enough. We'll call it... the spot."

A knowing smile crept across the shadowy figure's face, his eyes gleaming with satisfaction. The wheels were set in motion, and with excitement and apprehension, Gabriel was about to embark on a new journey that promised untold riches through the manipulation of a broken healthcare system.

As Gabriel delved deeper into healthcare fraud, he discovered the intricate mechanics behind this perfect crime. A key element that set this operation apart was the involvement of people from Cuba being recruited in the Miami area; these individuals wanted to return to their country and money to survive the hostile government.

Once the individuals were recruited, they would open medical supply companies in their names. Gabriel and Michael would open up a separate telemarketing service to call the elderly and offer them low-cost medical equipment; at that point, the elderly would give them the beneficiary numbers to bill the government agencies. and insurance companies for equipment and services. Michael, with his connections in the medical field, would give kickbacks to doctors willing to prescribe these patients equipment or services. Other ways that the syndicate got their patients was through social workers and elderly facilities.

Meanwhile, At the downtown Miami headquarters, the captain of the Miami task force called a stand-up meeting to address the alarming wave of fraudulent activities sweeping the city.

"Gentlemen, we are facing a strategic maneuver by these criminals that is baffling even our most seasoned investigators," the captain began. "The level of sophistication and coordination in these fraud schemes is unprecedented. We need our best minds on this, which is why I'm creating a specialized team to tackle these cases head-on."

Introducing the newly formed TUFF (Tactical Unit for Fraud), the Captain paired up two seasoned detectives Julian Pratt and Jackie Ortiz to lead the charge.

Julian 5'11" 38yearold, white man of average build,

was a seasoned detective hailing from South Carolina. A recently retired Navy veteran, his extensive experience made him an invaluable asset.

Partnered with him was Jackie Ortiz 5'8" 36yearold, fit Latina with black hair. Born and raised in South Florida, she had intimate knowledge of the city's underbelly and the types of schemes that flourished in the region.

As the investigation unfolded, a sense of frustration gripped the detectives. They found themselves caught in a web of deception, struggling to apprehend those responsible for the fraud. While not entirely in vain, their efforts primarily captured doctors, nurses, and other professionals involved in the scheme.

The trail of evidence led them through a maze of shell companies, offshore accounts, and carefully crafted alibis. Every time they thought they had a breakthrough, the perpetrators seemed to stay one step ahead, covering their tracks with ruthless efficiency.

Interrogations revealed a complex network of corruption, with individuals from various walks of life colluding to bilk the system. Physicians had falsified diagnoses, nurses had forged prescriptions, and administrators had embezzled funds, all in the pursuit of personal gain.

As the investigation dragged on, the detectives grew increasingly frustrated by the bureaucratic obstacles and legal loopholes that hindered their progress. They knew the true architects of the fraud were likely living lavish lifestyles, untouched by the consequences of their actions.

As Gabriel continued to build his empire within the healthcare fraud scheme, he became increasingly aware of the detectives' pursuit of these types of crimes. He reveled in the catandmouse game; his ego grew with each successful operation. Yet, he knew that the day of reckoning would eventually come. The knowledge that he and his cohorts were beyond the grasp of the law within the United States gave him a sense of invincibility, but it also fueled his insatiable desire for greater power and security.

Simultaneously, a dedicated task force assembled, their sole mission to unearth the truth behind the intricate web of deceit woven by the criminal syndicate. The task force comprised seasoned detectives, each determined to bring down the criminals behind the healthcare fraud scheme that plagued the city.

As the investigation unfolded, Julian Pratt and Jackie Ortiz began to uncover the true extent of the syndicate's ingenuity. They marveled at the meticulous planning and the flawless execution of fraudulent operations that had remained hidden in obscurity for far too long. The criminals had made fortunes fueled by greed, exploiting the vulnerabilities within the healthcare system to line their pockets with ill-gotten gains.

But the detectives were not easily deterred. They meticulously pieced together the evidence, connecting the dots that revealed the syndicate's modus operandi. As they dug deeper, they discovered a network of doctors, medical offices, and professionals complicit in the scheme, each arrest brought them closer to the core of the criminal organization and the depth of the corruption in this city.

They knew that to bring down these cunning criminals, they had to adapt their investigative strategies, think outside the box, and find alternative avenues to pierce through their fortress of deception.

It was no longer a mere chase; it had transformed into an elegant battle of chess, where the grandest of maneuvers would determine the victor. The team huddled, analyzing every angle and every possible move the criminals could make. They realized conventional methods would not suffice they needed to be as cunning and unpredictable as their targets.

Scouring through mountains of data, they began to uncover patterns, tiny cracks in the criminals' intricate web. Slowly, methodically, they laid the groundwork, setting the stage for a masterful trap. The anticipation was palpable, the stakes higher than ever before.

Chapter 2

GABRIEL'S SYNDICATE

Gabriel and Michael sat in a strip club, their usual spot. Gabriel, ever the cautious one, positioned himself facing the door with his back against the wall, constantly alert and scanning his surroundings.

This was their usual haunt in the heart of Miami, which pulsed with vibrant energy and activity.

The air was thick with the aroma of strong cigar smoke and the alluring scent of women's perfume, but beneath the surface, there was an undercurrent of something more sinister. Gabriel and Michael were not here for the entertainment they had darker intentions in mind.

They were there for a sit-down, a meeting. Gabriel felt comfortable talking in a loud room, which made it harder for anyone to listen or record the conversation.

Michael spoke just above a whisper, his words laden with anticipation. "Gabriel, it's the key to unlocking a new world of possibilities. We can bring people from Cuba to the United States and seamlessly return them without ever facing legal repercussions."

"This will give us the upper hand on our competitors and put us in a much better position. We don't have to recruit people in Miami to open the medical offices this will add an extra layer of protection, putting us further away from any type of investigation."

Gabriel nodded, his gaze unwaveringly fixed on Michael. "And how do we make this happen?"

Michael's eyes gleamed with a wicked glint. "We're going to be introduced to a government official from the island. He has the power to facilitate our plan. We'll meet him in Cuba and discuss the details."

"I was contacted by Juan Aguilar. This individual was among our first initial office proprietors whom we sent back to the Caribbean Island of Cuba. While in Cuba, he established connections with family members in the military, who were willing to collaborate in criminal activities. Their involvement included facilitating the departure of individuals from the island for a fee and allowing their return once their illicit activities were concluded. Juan Aguilar reached out to me to arrange a meeting with a Cuban government official, setting the stage for their nefarious endeavors."

Upon talking with Juan Aguilar, Michael found that he was the same person driven by ambition, unafraid, and always willing to take risks. The office owner, Juan Aguilar, had firsthand experience with the corrupt practices of the healthcare system and was more than willing to help exploit its vulnerabilities.

Juan Aguilar still harbored a strong desire for wealth and power, having seen how the system enriched the few at the expense of the many. He knew the risks were high, but the potential rewards were even higher.

Months of careful negotiations and arrangements culminated in the meeting Gabriel and Michael were about to attend. Once a vital figure in their criminal empire, the office owner had paved the way for this introduction. Through his connections and influence, he had secured them an audience with the elusive government official—an opportunity that could propel their illegal operations to unprecedented heights.

The day hung heavy with anticipation as Gabriel and Michael found themselves in the lavish surroundings of a resort in Varadero, Cuba. The sun cast a golden glow over the pristine beaches, but their minds were preoccupied with the meeting that awaited them.

As they settled into a corner of the resort's opulent restaurant, their attention was caught by a figure entering the room. Tall and imposing, he exuded an air of authority that commanded respect.

His thick mustache accentuated his stern expression, and his deep voice reverberated.

Accompanying him were two burly bodyguards, their eyes constantly scanning the surroundings, ever vigilant. Their presence sent a clear message: this man was not to be trifled with.

The restaurant, bustling with tourists and vacationers, suddenly fell silent as the official and his entourage approached Gabriel and Michael's table. Heads turned, whispers spread, and curious glances were exchanged. The aura of power emanating from the official created an atmosphere of curiosity and unease.

Without a word, the official signaled to his bodyguards. Swiftly and efficiently, they discreetly escorted the visitors to a secluded backroom of the exclusive resort. The dimly lit space was far removed from prying eyes and ears, ensuring no unwanted disruptions would interfere with the clandestine meeting about to take place.

Gabriel and Michael took their seats across from the

official, an air of anticipation and unease hanging thick in the room. The official wasted no time getting down to business, his voice low and measured as he outlined the delicate nature of the negotiations at hand.

Gabriel and Michael exchanged glances; their anticipation heightened. This was no ordinary meeting. The official's meticulous attention to detail and the power he commanded only served to underscore the gravity of their undertaking.

"This plan is very simple," he said, his voice low and gravelly, sending shivers down their spines. "I will arrange for our citizens to flee to the U.S., complete their mission, and then return to the island, living their lives untouched by prying eyes."

Gabriel's curiosity was piqued, and he couldn't help but inquire, "But how will they leave the island without detection?"

The government official smirked, revealing a cunning intelligence. "We'll meet off the coast of Cuba. My officers will be waiting on a boat at the designated point. And they will return the same way. It ensures you bypass immigration and have no records of leaving the U.S. Remember, money is bulky, and it's hard to travel with it on an airplane. The risk of losing the funds is too high. No flight manifests, no scrutiny. It's foolproof."

Gabriel's mind whirred with the implications of this operation. "And how many individuals can we transport?"

"As many as needed," the official replied, his eyes glinting with greed. "Our objective is to make as much money as possible quickly. With your help, we can achieve that."

Gabriel couldn't believe his luck. He had stumbled upon an opportunity beyond his wildest dreams. A smile played on his lips as he responded, "We have a deal."

On their return flight to Miami, Gabriel and Michael huddled together, their minds consumed with the scheme they had devised. They believed they had found the perfect way to exploit the healthcare and insurance system without raising suspicion. The key was to acquire the medical cards or insurance numbers of elderly patients and bill for fake services while remaining untraceable. They revealed they didn't need medical professionals or patients to execute their plan. This is 100% profit. No one has done this before. We are doing our way and cutting out all the middle people.

Gabriel's voice was low and calculated as he outlined their ideas. "We need a team of talented individuals, but not just anyone. We need people who are loyal to us and our cause. They will be our filter, shielding us from the arms of the law." A few weeks passed, and their new plan was set in motion. People started arriving from the island, eager to participate in the Miami syndicate plan.

Gabriel and Michael carefully selected individuals with the necessary skills and loyalty. They were meticulous in their recruitment process, ensuring they could trust those who would become an integral part of PMC.

They had connections within the medical industry, individuals who were ready for a change. These connections provided them with patient information, but it wasn't enough, they needed more. Gabriel, the mastermind behind the scheme, decided to open two to three medical supply offices every two months, each serving as a front for their illicit activities. These offices posed as legitimate businesses, but behind closed doors, they billed the healthcare system for millions of dollars' worth of services and equipment they never provided.

Gabriel reveled in the power he wielded, the wealth pouring into his coffers at an unimaginable rate. The syndicate's operations spanned the city, with dozens of offices generating millions of dollars each month. They lived in opulence, basking in their ill-gotten gains. Expensive jewelry adorned their bodies, exotic cars adorned their driveways, and exclusive clubs and restaurants welcomed them with open arms.

Money was no longer a constraint but a tool to fuel their desires. They were the envy of Miami, the talk of the town. The criminal empire they had built seemed unstoppable, their reputation growing with each passing day.

Chapter 3

DANCING IN LOVE'S EMBRACE

Gabriel and his friends reveled in the vibrant atmosphere of the upscale club, a renowned hots-pot for Miami's elite. The thumping bass reverberated through the air, the dance floor pulsated with bodies moving in sync with the rhythm, and the soft glow of colorful lights illuminated the space. It was a playground for the wealthy and influential, where decadence and indulgence were the norms.

Gabriel stood at the edge of the VIP section, surveying the scene with a practiced eye. Dressed impeccably in a tailored midnight blue suit accentuating his muscular frame, the suit, adorned with a sleek black tie, hinted at his sophistication and commanded attention wherever he went.

His eyes roamed the club, taking in the sights and sounds. The walls, adorned with modern art pieces, added a touch of elegance to the sleek and contemporary ambiance. The air was tinged with the scent of expensive perfumes and the clinking of glasses, creating an intoxicating atmosphere. The dance floor pulsed with the beat of the music, bodies swaying in a sensual rhythm. Amid the swirling colors and flashing lights, Gabriel's gaze became transfixed on a vision of allure across the crowded bar.

Her voluptuous Latina frame was accentuated by a figure-hugging white dress that seemed to mold to her every curve. Silky blonde hair cascaded down her shoulders, framing a face alive with a mischievous sparkle in her eyes and a sultry, seductive smile.

As he walked through the crowd, he caught fleeting glimpses of Sophia's infectious and radiant smile as she engaged in animated conversation with her friends. Her laughter blended seamlessly with the music, filling the air with a melodic symphony.

Finally reaching the bar, Gabriel positioned himself beside Sophia, his voice laced with confidence as he introduced himself. The clinking of glasses and the energetic conversations supported their encounter. Turning her gaze towards Gabriel, her eyes met his with curiosity and amusement. Sophia's beauty was captivating, accentuated by her flawless complexion and crimson lips that promised untold secrets.

Gabriel couldn't help but be drawn in by Sophia's magnetic presence. He complimented her, praising her beauty and charm, offering an invitation to join him and his friends in the VIP section. His voice carried a hint of intrigue, an invitation to indulge in a night of luxury and excitement. Sophia's friends exchanged knowing glances, mirroring her intrigue and adding an element of playful anticipation.

Intrigued by Gabriel's audacity and captivated by his charm, Sophia accepted his invitation. She gracefully led her friends toward the VIP section, exuding confidence and grace. Gabriel's friends welcomed them with open arms, their cheers resonating through the space as they celebrated the arrival of their new companions.

The night unfolded in a whirlwind of music, laughter, and champagne. Gabriel and Sophia danced, their bodies moving in perfect harmony, lost in the rhythm of the music. Their conversations flowed effortlessly, their connection growing stronger with every passing moment. It was a night of intoxicating energy and shared experiences.

As the DJ played on, casting a spell of enchantment over the crowded dance floor, Gabriel pulled Sophia close, her delicate frame fitting against his, finally united. The air was tense, a magnetic pull that had been building since the moment they first laid eyes on each other.

Sophia's heart raced as Gabriel's fingers traced the curve of her waist, his touch igniting a fire within her. Feeling a desperate need to be closer to him, to feel the warmth of his body against hers, Sophia reached up, threading her fingers through his hair and pulling him down until their lips met in a passionate kiss. It was a kiss that conveyed all the unspoken feelings they had been harboring.

She gazed up at him, her eyes sparkling with a mixture of desire and wonderment. At that moment, nothing else mattered – not the pulsing music, not the chatter of the guests, not the flowing champagne. There was only Gabriel and Sophia, caught in a passionate embrace.

Time seemed to stand still as they moved as one, their bodies swaying and twisting in a dance of unbridled passion. Every brush of skin, every heated glance, every whispered word fueled the growing intensity between Gabriel and Sophia.

Hands intertwined, they stumbled to Gabriel's Porsche and drove through the dimly lit streets of Miami, fueled by the unbridled passion that had ignited between them at the club. The pulsing beats and swaying bodies had set Gabriel and Sophia's blood on fire, and now all they craved was to be alone, to feel each other's touch uninhibited.

Breathless, they crashed through Gabriel's apartment door, unable to keep their hands off one another. Clothes were hastily discarded, falling to the floor in a trail towards the bedroom. Moonlight streamed in through the panoramic windows of Gabriel's apartment, casting a silvery glow over their tangled limbs as Sophia fell back onto the bed in a tangle of desperate kisses and caressing fingertips.

The city of Miami lights twinkled below, a backdrop to their fervent exploration of each other's bodies. Gabriel's hands mapped Sophia's curves, igniting sparks that threatened to consume them. Sighs and gasps mingled as Gabriel and Sophia gave in to the primal need burning within them, driven by an all-consuming passion.

Muscles tensed and relaxed, skin slick with sweat as they moved together, lost in a world of their creation. Time seemed to slow, every touch and sensation heightened, intensifying the pleasure that built and built until it crested in a series of trembling, ecstatic releases.

Spent, they clung to one another, heartbeats slowly returning to normal as they reveled in the afterglow, gazing out at the glittering cityscape below. At that moment, nothing else mattered but the connection Gabriel and Sophia shared, a bond forged in the heat of passion that would forever be etched into their memories.

As the hours waned and the sun began to peek over the

horizon, Gabriel and Sophia were engrossed in each other's presence. Their bond had deepened, their souls entwined amidst the flickering lights and pulsating beats. They felt as though they had known each other for a lifetime, their connection transcending the boundaries of time and space.

Gabriel woke early, planting a gentle kiss on Sophia's forehead before slipping out of bed. "Sleep in a little longer, baby girl," he whispered. "I'll make us a special breakfast."

In the kitchen, Gabriel moved with practiced ease, preparing his favorite dishes. The aroma of freshly brewed Cuban coffee and sizzling bacon soon filled the air, making Sophia's mouth water. When the table was set, Gabriel returned to the bedroom.

"Breakfast is ready," he announced softly, placing a tray across Sophia's lap. "Enjoy, and don't worry about a thing. This is our moment to relax."

Smiling up at Gabriel, Sophia saw the contentment in his eyes. They savored the meal together, the world outside fading away as they indulged in this peaceful respite.

However, the tranquility was soon interrupted when Gabriel's phone rang, and he recognized Michael's urgent voice on the other end. The call brought news of a smuggling operation going wrong, with the cargo of three recruits for their healthcare office, at risk.

As Michael explained the situation with the boat

running low on fuel, Gabriel's mind raced to find a solution. The success of their smuggling operation relied on smooth coordination and quick thinking. With determination, Gabriel laid out a plan.

"Michael, contact the captain on the satellite phone, providing new coordinates. Tell him to go to our emergency point is the old abandoned dock. This would allow the captain to safely approach a remote location and rendezvous with one of our syndicate members. The crew member could then refuel the boat, ensuring it had enough to make it to Miami without raising any suspicion."

Time was of the essence, and Michael quickly passed along the updated coordinates to the captain. The captain acknowledged the message and altered course, navigating stealthily toward the new meeting location.

Right after hanging up, Michael immediately contacted Jorge Acosta. In his 60s with grey hair and a bit on the heavy side, Jorge lived in the Florida Keys. A fisherman by trade who knew his way around, he was the guy down south who was closest to the meeting point. Michael explained in a low tone what they needed.

Jorge replied without hesitation, "I'm on it. A bit risky, I would say, a daytime operation." He assured Michael he would gather the recruits and have them dropped off to Raphael Santos in Miami. Raphael, in his 30s and nicknamed Chino, was a Cuban Asian who grew up in

Havana's Chinatown neighborhood. He was under Michael, making him third in command in the Miami syndicate, and was in charge of getting the recruits and the office ready for business.

Jorge hurried down to the old boatyard with worn-down docks, where the speedboat was waiting. As it pulled up, the crew quickly topped off the fuel tanks, making sure they had enough fuel to make the run to Miami without stops. Within minutes, the boat was loaded up and ready to continue its journey to the final point.

Jorge looked around nervously, hoping they hadn't attracted any unwanted attention. But the dock was quiet, and the boat sped off into the open waters, leaving no trace behind.

Jorge looked over at the recruit, a young Cuban man no older than twenty-five, holding the door handle. The boatyard faded in the rear-view mirror as they merged onto the highway and headed north to Miami.

"Relax, kid," Jorge said in his scratchy but reassuring voice. "Chino, the man you're going to spend many months with, is a hard-ass, but he's a man of his word. Do as he says, and you'll be rolling in cash before you know it."

The recruit swallowed hard, giving a small, worried smirk. Jorge could smell the fear radiating off him, that potent mix of excitement and uncertainty that every new hire has. It didn't matter their background—gang banger, jar-head, or just some punk looking for easy money—they all got that rabbit-in-the-headlights look when the reality of doing something illegal set in.

But Raphael (Chino) had a way of separating the weak from the strong. Raphael was in charge of getting the recruits and the office ready for business. The Miami Syndicate operations had grown bolder and more lucrative. The jobs got more intense, sure, but the payouts were enough to make a man risk his freedom. Jorge had been with the Miami syndicate long enough to know that the ends always justified the means in this line of work.

As Jorge's van rumbled down the streets of Miami's warehouse district, the humid air thickened. His hands were firmly on the steering wheel as he navigated rundown buildings, always looking in the rear-view mirror at the two nervous faces seated on the floor in the back of the van and the younger kid seated next to him.

He pulled up to a nondescript warehouse, the rusted metal door barely hanging on its hinges. Jorge killed the engine and stepped out, motioning for the others to follow.

As they approached the entrance, a stocky figure emerged from inside—Raphael, known as "el Chino" to the recruits. A sly smile spread across his face as he clapped Jorge on the back.

"Job well done, my brother," Raphael said with a gravelly voice. He produced a thick envelope, pressing it into Jorge's hand. "For your job."

Jorge thanked him, the weight of the cash a familiar comfort. He'd been running this route for years with other drug organizations, and now he was on the payroll for the Miami syndicate. He was just a call away, no questions asked.

Raphael turned to the wide-eyed group, his look cold. "Welcome to the USA and your new life, my friends."

As Raphael (alias Chino) gathered the group of fresh recruits, their eyes wide with a mix of anticipation and nerves, he scanned the faces before him, sizing up the newest additions to the operation.

"All right, listen up," he said, his tone casual but firm. "I need each of you to give me the address where you'll be staying—with family, friends, whoever. Just make sure it's secure."

One by one, they provided the details, and Raphael jotted them down in his well-worn notebook. With a nod, he motioned for them to follow him to his Range Rover.

As they piled in, Raphael (Chino) slid behind the wheel, glancing over his shoulder before peeling away from the curb. "Here's how it's gonna work," he began, keeping his eyes on the road. "I'll be reaching out to each of you in the next couple of days to go over the operation. Details, roles, the whole nine yards."

He paused, making sure they were following. "But here's the thing—you don't breathe a word of this to anyone. Not your mama, not your best friend, no one. This shit is highly illegal, and you never know who you might be talking to."

The van slowed as they approached the first dropoff point. "Got it?" Raphael (Chino) fixed the young recruit with a pointed stare, waiting for the nervous nod before continuing. He handed him a cell phone. "This is how I will reach you. Keep it on you at all times."

One by one, he deposited them at their temporary houses, the same warning on his lips each time. As the last recruit disappeared behind a nondescript door, Raphael allowed himself a tight smile. If they made it through the initiation, they'd be worth the investment made.

Later that evening, the carefully orchestrated plan was executed flawlessly, leaving them relieved that they had averted a potential disaster. Gabriel knew there was little time for celebration, as the world they navigated demanded constant vigilance and adaptability.

As the moon ascended, its silver light casting a serene glow over the city, Gabriel and Sophia found themselves wrapped in a moment of pure connection. The night air, alive with the subtle rhythms of the city, seemed to celebrate their union, each whispering a testament to the timeless romance. In the sanctuary of the balcony, the couple's shared gaze spoke volumes, their silent communication more profound than words could ever convey. The world, with all its chaos and clamor, melted away, leaving only the truth of their shared affection, as enduring and luminous as the moon above.

In the quiet solitude of his reflection, Gabriel's resolve hardened like steel. He understood the weight of his lifestyle that trailed his every step, the silent witnesses to a life fringed with danger. Yet, in Sophia's eyes, he saw the promise of redemption, a beacon of innocence that he vowed to protect. It was a silent oath, etched deep within his heart, to shield her from the tempest of his world. For in her laughter, he found hope, and in her dreams, the strength to forge a new path—one where the specters of his past would no longer cast their dark veil over their future.

Gabriel's fingers traced the delicate curve of Sophia's cheek; his touch made her smile and gave her a sense of security. It was a simple gesture, but one that carried immense weight in their relationship.

Staring at his reflection, Gabriel made a silent promise to himself. He would keep Sophia at a distance from his illicit activities, ensuring her safety and preserving the purity of their love. She deserved a life untouched by the phantoms that haunted him, where she could thrive and be free from the consequences of his choices.

His enemies were ruthless, always searching for weaknesses to exploit. Gabriel couldn't risk exposing Sophia to their malicious intentions. He had seen the lengths they would go to; the lives they had destroyed. Sophia was his sanctuary, the light that guided him through the darkness. He couldn't bear the thought of that light being extinguished.

Sophia looked into his eyes, seeing the unwavering love and dedication in his gaze. Though questions still lingered in her mind, she took comfort in his words and the strength of their connection.

"I trust you, Gabriel," she replied, her voice filled with love and determination. "As long as we're together, we can face anything that comes our way."

A few days had gone by. Raphael (Chino) scanned over the trio of recruits: a wiry young man with curly hair, a skinny man in his late twenties with sharp features and a no-nonsense demeanor, and an older gentleman with graying hair but a fiery determination burning in his eyes.

"All right, listen up," Raphael's (Chino's) gruff voice carried over the dull roar of the engine. "This isn't some walk in the park. The operation we're about to undertake is dangerous, demanding, and there's no guarantee of success. If any of you want to back out, now's the time."

The trio exchanged looks, their jaws set in silent resolution. Chino smirked, seemingly impressed by their conviction. "Don't worry, I know this is all new territory for you, but you wanted this mission because of your will to make money, dedication, and sacrifice to be here."

He began explaining the operation's objectives: first and foremost, they were not to discuss their operations with anyone outside the organization. Absolute secrecy was a must.

"Secondly, I'm going to send you to a lawyer's office that specializes in handling the necessary paperwork to obtain your work permits. This will speed up the process of your documentation so we can open our medical supply business."

"Third, you will need to form a corporation, a legal entity to serve as a front for our illicit activities. This will lend an air of credibility and legitimacy to the operation."

Raphael's voice carried a harsh tone as he addressed his new team, emphasizing the critical nature of their upcoming fraudulent operation. Every member understood the gravity of the situation, their faces etched with determination. "We have one chance to get this right," Raphael (Chino) said. "The success of this operation hinges on our ability to follow the plan meticulously. Failure is not an option."

Over the next few months, Raphael (alias el Chino) coordinated every aspect—providing documentation, following up relentlessly, and ensuring no stone was left unturned. The lawyers worked tirelessly.

Chapter 4

THE BALANCING ACT

Amidst the bustling streets of Miami, the diverse and vibrant cityscape provided a backdrop for the expanding operation led by Gabriel and his team. As their reach extended, the intricate web of their enterprise began to intertwine with the lives of individuals from different backgrounds and walks of life.

Omar Garcia, a young Cuban immigrant in his 30s with a dark complexion who stood at 5'9", was one of the earlier recruits brought to Miami from Cuba to open an illegal medical supply office. He was just the owner on paper that the Miami syndicate needed to establish a medical supply office that would serve as a front for fraudulently billing operations in the healthcare system and private insurance companies, profiting millions in a few months.

He spoke broken English—an unassuming figure in the illicit world of healthcare fraud. Yet, he was about to be pulled into a web of deceit and greed that would test the very limits of his morals.

The promise of wealth and a lavish lifestyle had initially seduced Omar, feeding his long-held dreams of prosperity. Coming from a humble background, the allure of the "easy money" offered by the Miami Syndicate seemed like a tantalizing escape from the constraints of his past.

Drawn in by the relentless pursuit of financial gain, Omar found himself entangled in a complex scheme targeting the healthcare system. The prospect of a life of luxury back in Cuba was tempting. However, as time went on, Omar's perspective shifted. The vibrant energy of Miami and the freedom he experienced within the United States began to reveal a different side of life—a world where opportunities abounded, dreams could be pursued, and one's worth was measured beyond material wealth.

Caught between the enticing promises of the operation and the newfound appreciation for the liberties he had come to cherish, Omar found himself at a crossroads. The allure of ill-gotten riches clashed with a growing sense of morality, a voice that whispered of the consequences that awaited those who chose a path of deceit and fraud.

Weighing the scales of his desires against the potential repercussions, Omar grappled with the secrecy of his thoughts. The realization that his involvement in the fraudulent billing scheme carried the risk of tarnishing his newfound life gnawed at his conscience. He yearned for the stability and security of Miami, the chance to build a legitimate future based on merit rather than deception.

Despite the allure, doubts began to consume Omar. The city's vibrant colors seemed muted, tainted by the dishonesty that permeated his actions. The taste of freedom he relished was tainted by the knowledge that it rested on a foundation of fraud.

Seeking solace and guidance, Omar confided in a fellow associate, sharing the doubts that clouded his conscience. The associate, well aware of the moral complexity of their operations, understood the weight of Omar's concerns. Together, they contemplated the paths before them, evaluating the consequences of their choices and seeking a resolution that would bring clarity to their murky circumstances.

Realizing the gravity of the situation, the associate decided to involve Raphael, their trusted confidante. Raphael met with Omar, listening to his concerns and recognizing the delicate balance that needed to be maintained.

The atmosphere in Raphael's office was heavy with anticipation as he sat across from the troubled Cuban recruit. Raphael's piercing gaze met Omar's eyes, conveying understanding and determination.

"I appreciate you coming to me with your concerns," Raphael began, his voice carrying a soothing yet authoritative tone. "It takes courage to question the path you've been set upon."

Omar's shoulders sagged with the weight of his conflicted emotions. " Raphael, I never imagined myself in this situation. The life I had dreamt of in Miami didn't involve deception and fraud. But I feel trapped, torn between the promises of wealth and the desire for a life built on truth."

Raphael leaned forward, resting his forearms on the worn wooden surface of his desk. "I understand the struggles you're facing. It's not an easy decision, but I assure you, we will find a way to resolve this without compromising your wellbeing."

Hope flickered in Omar's eyes as he searched for reassurance. "But what can we do, Raphael? How can I step away from this scheme without facing dire consequences?"

A devious smirk played on Michael's lips as he reached out, placing a comforting hand on Omar's arm. "We must be cautious and strategic. The key is to navigate this path delicately, ensuring the least disruption to our operations while honoring your desire for a different future."

Omar nodded, his faith in Raphael growing stronger. "I trust your judgment, Raphael. Please guide me through this; help me find a way out."

Raphael's voice took on a measured tone, his words laced with determination. "Rest assured; we will handle this with utmost care. I will confer with our contacts and devise a plan that allows you to step away without endangering yourself or our operation."

But Omar had had enough. For years, he had been entrenched in the shadowy world of the Miami Syndicate, a life of deceit, violence, and constant fear. But now, he wanted out. He dreamed of a legitimate future, one where he could leave and start a new life in Miami.

It had taken months of careful planning, but finally, Omar had managed to extricate himself from the syndicate's grip. He was ready to disappear into the anonymity of regular life, or so he thought.

Within weeks, Omar's dreams of a fresh start were shattered. As he walked down a side street in Miami, a van screeched to a halt beside him. Before he could react, strong hands grabbed him, and he was bundled into the vehicle, his cries for help muffled by the roar of the engine.

Omar knew only one crew could be behind this – the

Miami Syndicate he had failed to keep his agreement with just weeks earlier. The syndicate had long memories, and Omar had broken a sacred trust, owing them money for his transport to Miami from Cuba. Now, he would have to face the consequences.

As the van sped through the city streets, Omar's heart pounded in his chest. He knew his fate was sealed. The syndicate would not let him go so easily, and he braced himself for the horrors that lay ahead. The dream of a normal life had been just that a dream. Omar's past had caught up with him, and now he would have to fight for his very survival.

Omar had always been a bit of a risk-taker, but this time he had gotten himself into a mess. He had agreed with the PMC but failed to keep his side of the deal, thinking it would be a simple way out of his agreement. Little did he know, that as they drove towards the docks, Omar started to get an uneasy feeling in his stomach. The PMC were silent and focused, their expressions unreadable. When they arrived and he saw the sleek, off-shore-powered boat waiting for them, alarm bells started going off in his head.

"Where exactly are we going?" he asked, trying to keep his voice steady.

One of the PMC guys turned to him with a cold stare. "Cuba." Omar's mind raced. What the hell had he gotten himself into? He knew the PMC had connections there, but he had no idea they were going to smuggle him out of Miami and back to Cuba. His fate was now completely out of his control.

As they boarded the boat and sped away into the night, Omar sat in grim silence, his heart pounding. He had a sinking feeling that this was a one-way trip and that his life would never be the same. The cold, calculating looks on the faces of his "companions" made it clear that there was no backing out now.

In the quiet moments between the frenetic activity, Gabriel and Michael would reflect on the journey that had brought them to this point. They were proud of what they had built, but they also recognized the fragility of it all. One misstep, one moment of weakness, and everything could come crashing down.

As the PMC continued to thrive, Gabriel remained vigilant, knowing that each challenge presented an opportunity. On the streets of Miami, the PMC was built on trust and respect, a delicate balance that he fought to maintain amidst the chaos.

A few days later, Raphael and Michael convened their weekly meeting, a routine gathering where they discussed the intricate details of their fraudulent operations. The air was thick with tension as they dug into the recent developments following the Omar Garcia incident.

Michael wasted no time addressing the pressing matter, his tone laced with urgency. "So, what's the status of the profit monies collected through our fraudulent activities?"

Raphael opened his briefcase and retrieved his notepad. Michael's eyes scanned the figures before him as Raphael explained, "We've managed to take out of the bank this week over eight hundred thousand from a couple of medical supply offices." His voice was low and calculated.

"Michael, we have a little more than three million dollars remaining in the banks as of today, and lots more funds hitting the bank next week to take out. We need more resources to extract the money. This is just from two offices; we should be opening three more medical offices in the next few months."

Michael raised his head slightly as Raphael laid out the numbers. "Three million left to extract, huh? Our currency exchange connection better step up his game. He used to take out one million a week for us; why has he slowed down?"

"He's doing what he can without raising too many flags for now," Raphael replied. "Once we get the other three medical offices running, we will double our profit stream."

Michael leaned back, running a hand through his hair. This money laundering operation was more complicated than anticipated, but the profits from funneling illegal gains through legitimate businesses were too substantial to abandon now.

"Okay, we'll stick with the current connection we have for now, but keep vetting some alternates. I don't want any choke-points when we're doing so well," Michael instructed, his jaw set. They had invested too much to allow a single weak link to slow down the operation.

Chapter 5

DECEPTION AND EXPLOITATION

Gabriel and Sophia's weeks after their first meeting were a frenzy of love and desire. It felt like they were caught in a current, carrying them effortlessly through a series of magical moments that seemed straight out of a fairy tale.

Every date they shared was carefully planned, each detail meticulously thought out to create an enchanting experience for both. Gabriel, always the epitome of charm, would arrive at Sophia's doorstep in his sleek, red Porsche, a dazzling smile illuminating his face. The sight of him never failed to make her heart skip a beat. With a tender embrace and a whispered compliment, they would embark on their adventure for the day.

Their journeys together took them to hidden gems throughout the city, known only to those willing to explore beyond the beaten path. Hand in hand, they roamed through picturesque parks, relishing the beauty of nature unfolding before their eyes. They shared laughter, engaged in lighthearted banter, and reveled in the joy of being together.

And when the evening fell, their dates transformed into elegant affairs that awakened the senses. Gabriel would sweep Sophia off her feet, leading her into candlelit restaurants adorned with exquisite décor. The aroma of tantalizing dishes mingled with their laughter, creating an ambiance that enveloped them in their world. Time seemed to stand still as they savored delectable delicacies, engaging in deep conversations that challenged their minds and opened their hearts.

But their love truly flourished in the intimate moments behind closed doors. Gabriel's luxurious apartment became a sanctuary, a haven where they could escape from the outside world and lose themselves in their desires. Soft music filled the air, and the flickering candles cast a warm, sensual glow on their entwined bodies.

In those stolen moments of intimacy, they discovered a language that words could not express. Their bodies moved in perfect harmony, their fingertips tracing delicate patterns on each other's skin, igniting a fire that consumed them both. They surrendered to the passion that simmered between them, the symphony of their love creating a crescendo that echoed throughout the room. Time seemed to lose all meaning as they surrendered to the waves of pleasure, lost in a world where only their connection mattered.

But it wasn't just physical desire that bound them together. In the safety of each other's embrace, they found the courage to reveal their deepest fears and insecurities. They shared stories of their pasts, the scars they carried, and the battles they had fought. In those moments of vulnerability, they found solace and understanding, offering each other unwavering support and acceptance. Their bond transcended the physical, becoming an unbreakable union of hearts and souls.

As they lay in each other's arms, their bodies intertwined, they marveled at the beauty of their love. Their whispers filled the room with promises and declarations, affirming their unwavering commitment to one another. In those tender moments, they created a sanctuary to escape the world's chaos and find solace in each other's presence.

Together, they discovered a love that was profound and all-encompassing, a love that defied logic and surpassed their wildest dreams. In the embrace of Gabriel's apartment, they created memories that would forever be etched in their hearts. As they embarked on this journey of love, they knew without a doubt that they had found something extraordinary in each other.

As Gabriel and Sophia reveled in the depths of their love and passion, unaware of the impending storm looming outside the walls of Gabriel's apartment, the courtroom was filled with an air of anticipation. It was a stark contrast to the intimacy they shared.

Tension filled the air as U.S. Attorney Alice Harper, a 34yearold professional Black woman, along with lead detectives Julian Pratt and Jackie Ortiz, prepared to present their case before the judge. The stakes were high—they needed to secure indictments and search warrants for their suspects, cunning and elusive individuals who had evaded justice for far too long.

As they gathered their evidence and reviewed their strategy, Alice could feel the weight of responsibility on her shoulders. This was a pivotal moment that could make or break their case. She knew Julian and Jackie had put in countless hours, sifting through details, chasing down leads, and building a solid foundation to support their arguments.

The courtroom was tense with the weight of the alleged fraudulent activities that had cast a dark shadow over the healthcare system in South Florida. With meticulous precision, U.S. Attorney Alice Harper laid out the evidence, painting a vivid picture of the massive scam that had caused significant losses to taxpayers and undermined the integrity of the healthcare industry. Billing Medicare and private insurance for millions of dollars, these companies had exploited the system by charging for unnecessary or nonexistent medical equipment. The web of deceit extended its reach, connecting one suspect to another in an intricate fraud network. The judge granted the search and arrest warrants.

The early morning stillness was shattered by the thunderous crash of splintering doors as the TUFF team poured into the nondescript office building housing Gordon's medical office. "This is a raid! Get on the ground, now!" bellowed the lead agent Julian Pratt, his voice booming with authority.

Inside, a flurry of activity ensued as agents fanned out, securing the premises and rounding up the startled employees. In the back office, a white man in an ill-fitting suit, drops of sweat forming on his forehead, found himself pinned against the wall by two heavyset agents.

"Gordon Fisher, in his late 60s with gray hair, you're under arrest for healthcare fraud and money laundering," one of the agents growled, slapping cuffs on the man's wrists.

Meanwhile, across town, a separate team conducted a similar raid on the lavish mansion belonging to DD Medical's owner, Daniel Decker, a former high-school dropout turned millionaire, known for his flashy lifestyle and love of expensive toys.

As the TUFF agents swarmed his palatial estate, Decker attempted a mad dash for the exit, only to be tackled to the ground by the female agent Jackie Ortiz. "Going somewhere, Danny boy?" Jackie taunted as he was cuffed and dragged away.

The simultaneous raids were the culmination of years of investigation by U.S. Attorney Alice Harper and her team of professional law enforcement in Miami. The fraudulent schemes hatched by DD Medical and their cohorts had billed Medicare out of millions, leaving countless patients without proper care.

But as Harper surveyed the evidence being cataloged, a grim satisfaction settled over her. The TUFF team had struck a blow against the cancer of healthcare fraud, but she knew the battle was far from over. There would always be those willing to sacrifice integrity for greed.

Dr. Fisher's involvement in the scam sent shock-waves through the investigation. A respected figure in orthopedics, he had built a reputation on trust and care for his patients. The detectives couldn't help but wonder how someone so highly regarded could be entangled in activities causing significant losses to taxpayers.

As they delved deeper, the detectives uncovered

suspicious transactions and irregularities surrounding DD Medical Supply and Dr. Fisher's orthopedic office. They meticulously sifted through piles of documents, cross-referencing billing records and patient testimonials to gather the evidence needed to build their case.

Their efforts were not in vain. The puzzle pieces began to fall into place, revealing a complex scheme involving multiple parties. DD Medical Supply appeared to be billing Medicare and private insurance companies for millions of dollars' worth of unnecessary or nonexistent medical equipment. Meanwhile, Dr. Fisher's orthopedic office seemed complicit in the operation, potentially benefiting from the fraudulent transactions.

With each piece of evidence, they uncovered, the scope of the scam became increasingly apparent. Julian Pratt and Jackie Ortiz discovered a web of interconnected companies, each playing a role in the elaborate scheme to defraud the healthcare system. Among these entities was Mas Supply Inc., a relatively new company that had billed over $20 million in less than a year for dubious services. The audacity of their operations stunned even the most seasoned investigators.

Detectives Julian Pratt and Jackie Ortiz understood the gravity of their task. They were not only seeking justice for the taxpayers who had fallen victim to this massive scam but also aiming to restore the integrity of the healthcare system. The ripple effects of such widespread fraud extended beyond monetary losses; they undermined the trust between patients and healthcare providers, tarnishing the reputation of an industry built on the principle of care and healing.

As the task force carried out the raids on the suspected fraudulent medical supply companies, they encountered an unexpected obstacle at Mas Supply Inc. Their plan to catch the owner red-handed had been thwarted; he was nowhere to be found. Instead, they were greeted by a receptionist who seemed oblivious to the situation unfolding around her. Language proved to be another barrier, as she could only communicate in a language the detectives did not understand.

Undeterred by the language barrier, a Spanish-speaking detective stepped forward to bridge the gap. He calmly explained to the receptionist, in her native tongue, the purpose of their presence. With a mix of confusion and trepidation, she listened intently as the detective informed her that they were seizing documents and computers as evidence. He handed her a card and instructed her to pass along the message to her boss, urging him to contact the task force.

Despite the initial encounter, the task force leader couldn't shake the feeling that there was more to this seemingly innocuous office than met the eye. He had an unspoken intuition that the owner of Mas Supply Inc. was hiding something significant. Determined not to let potential leads slip through their fingers, he left a group of detectives behind at the office, patiently waiting for the owner's return.

As the investigation delved deeper into Mas Supply Inc., it became evident that this office was unlike any they had encountered. Julian Pratt and Jackie Ortiz meticulously questioned the doctors who allegedly prescribed supplies to countless patients associated with the company. Surprisingly, the doctors claimed not to know about Mas Supply Inc. It was as if the company existed solely in the shadows, operating without leaving a trace.

The puzzle pieces began to fall into place. The patients, too, had never received any supplies or services from Mas Supply Inc. They were left bewildered, their trust shattered, as they realized they had unwittingly become pawns in a scheme orchestrated by faceless manipulators. The promise of medical equipment had been dangled before them, enticing them to provide their personal and health information. The patients recounted their encounters with telemarketers who had contacted them, offering services that seemed too good to be true.

The detective listened intently as one patient, haunted by her experience, shared her story. She described the persuasive tactics employed by the telemarketers, their ability to extract personal details, and the false promises they made. Each word made it apparent that Mas Supplies Inc. had operated as a ghost company, preying on vulnerable individuals and exploiting the healthcare system for personal gain.

Unlike legitimate medical supply companies that diligently delivered equipment to beneficiaries, Mas Supplies Inc. had never shipped anything to anyone. They had cynically pocketed the funds for healthcare services, disappearing without a trace. The scale of the deception was staggering, as the investigation revealed a web of connections between doctors, their family members, and friends, all complicit in this intricate scheme.

The realization of Mas Supplies Inc.'s fraudulent activities sent shock-waves through the task force. They had encountered their fair share of illicit operations, but this one was particularly insidious. The company had operated with cunning and precision, leaving no room for detection. It was a stark reminder of the lengths to which individuals would go to exploit a system designed to provide care and support.

As the evidence against Mas Supplies Inc. mounted, the detectives meticulously documented each step of their investigation. They uncovered a trail of financial transactions, communication records, and witness testimonies that precisely unraveled the intricate scheme.

Their tireless efforts began to reveal the individuals behind the ghost company, though they knew the journey to bring them to justice would be arduous.

With the closure of Mas Supplies Inc., the task force had struck a significant blow against the fraudulent activities plaguing the healthcare system. Their work was far from over, but dismantling this ghost company marked a turning point in their pursuit of justice. The task force knew their findings would serve as a foundation to expose the wider network of deceit and manipulation threatening the integrity of the healthcare industry.

The patients, who had unwittingly become victims of Mas Supplies Inc.'s machinations, were left to grapple with the aftermath. Their trust had been shattered, and they now faced the daunting task of rebuilding their confidence in a system that had failed them. The investigation offered a glimmer of hope, a reassurance that those responsible would be held accountable and the healthcare system would be safeguarded from such egregious exploitation in the future.

As the task force methodically compiled their findings and prepared to present their case, they were fueled by a renewed sense of purpose. The exposure of Mas Supplies Inc. revealed the true nature of the fraud that had ensnared countless individuals and siphoned funds from the healthcare system. Their determination to bring justice to those involved burned brighter than ever as they pushed forward, committed to uncovering the full extent of this ghost company's operations and ensuring that the perpetrators faced the consequences of their actions.

The task force gathered in their conference room, the air electric with anticipation. Detective Jackie Ortiz, her eyes ablaze with determination, pinned the last piece of evidence to their sprawling investigation board.

"This is it, team," she declared, her voice trembling with barely contained passion. "We've got Mas Supplies Inc. cornered."

Detective Mike Reeves nodded, his weathered face etched with resolve. "It's been a long road, but we're finally going to expose these vultures for what they are."

As they rehearsed their presentation, the gravity of their discovery weighed heavily on each member. Mas Supplies Inc., a phantom company that had wormed its way into the healthcare system, had billed millions from unsuspecting victims and diverted crucial funds from those who needed it most.

The team worked tirelessly through the night, fueled by coffee and an unquenchable thirst for justice. They meticulously connected the dots, revealing a web of deceit that stretched far beyond what they had initially imagined.

Dawn broke as they put the finishing touches on their

case. Jackie stood before her colleagues, her voice quivering with emotion. "What we do today isn't just about numbers on a spreadsheet. It's about the lives destroyed, the trust shattered, and the system corrupted. We owe it to every victim to see this through."

As they called in their superiors and other task force members to present their findings, a fire burned in their hearts. The task force knew that this was more than just another case – it was a crusade against those who would prey on the vulnerable.

In the presentation room, faced with stern-faced officials, Detective Jackie Ortiz's passion ignited the room. She painted a vivid picture of Mas Supplies Inc.'s insidious operations, her words a rallying cry for justice.

With each revelation, the officials' expressions changed from skepticism to shock, then to fierce determination. The task force had not just built a case; they had sparked a movement.

As they concluded, a thunderous applause filled the room. Detective Reeves caught Agent Chen's eye, a silent understanding passing between them. This was only the beginning. They would pursue every lead, uncover every conspirator, and dismantle this fraudulent empire piece by piece.

The task force left the building, their steps light but

purposeful. They knew the challenges in front of them, but their resolve was unshakeable. For in their hands, they held the power to right a terrible wrong and restore faith in a system meant to heal, not harm.

Their fight against Mas Supplies Inc. had become more than an investigation – it was a testament to the enduring power of justice and the unwavering spirit of those who champion it.

Chapter 6

UNMASKING THE SYNDICATE

Detectives Julian Pratt and Jackie Ortiz followed a paper trail that led them through a maze of shell corporations, forged documents, and complex money laundering schemes. Slowly, they pieced together how these criminals systematically looted their victims and then disappeared before the authorities could close in.

What was most unsettling was the precision with which these owners orchestrated their disappearances. Bank accounts would be cleaned out, offices abandoned, and personal effects vanished—all within a matter of days. It was as if they had simply evaporated, leaving no clues behind.

The Miami Task Force pored over financial records, interviewed witnesses, and scoured digital devices, but each time they thought they had a lead, it would go cold. The owners had planned their escapes meticulously, covering their tracks at every turn.

As the investigation dragged on, Julian Pratt and Jackie Ortiz grew increasingly frustrated. They knew these criminals were still out there somewhere, enjoying the spoils of their ill-gotten gains. But without a single credible sighting or tangible evidence, apprehending them seemed an impossible task.

As their investigation intensified, their healthcare crime painted a sobering picture. They noticed that three out of every five of their fraud cases they encountered had a disturbingly common outcome—the responsible owners would vanish, leaving behind only the shattered dreams and devastated lives of their victims.

This reality underscored the immense challenge faced by Julian and Jackie. These criminals, driven by greed and a disregard for the wellbeing of others, meticulously planned their schemes, amassed ill-gotten gains, and then disappeared without a trace when their fraudulent activities were finally uncovered.

The victims, having trusted these unscrupulous

individuals with their life savings or investments, were left to pick up the pieces, often with little recourse or hope of recovering their losses. This pattern highlighted the need for stronger laws, better investigative tools, and greater collaboration between authorities to combat the growing epidemic of financial crimes.

Despite the sobering statistics, the Miami Task Force remained undeterred. Driven by a steadfast commitment to pursuing justice and holding these white-collar criminals accountable, the team knew their work, though arduous, was essential in providing closure and restitution for those whose lives had been devastated by the actions of these unscrupulous individuals.

Of the 15 individuals apprehended, four were potentially key players in a single enterprise operating within Dade County. These individuals were suspected of using four fictitious durable medical equipment companies to fraudulently charge the medical system a staggering $25 million for equipment never delivered to patients. The suspects and their offices fit the pattern the detectives had been pursuing, further solidifying their belief that they were part of the Miami syndicate organization.

With news of the arrests spreading, Gabriel quickly sprang into action. Aware of the significance of the upcoming arraignment, he contacted Michael. Their priority was to ensure that the four individuals had competent attorneys present during the court hearing, allowing them to secure a bond.

Time was of the essence, and Gabriel knew he had to move fast. He reached out to his network of criminal defense lawyers, explained the situation, and asked for their assistance. Several agreed to be at the hearing.

Meanwhile, the dedicated detectives meticulously combed through an overwhelming volume of documents, computers, and bank transactions seized during the raids. Each piece of evidence was scrutinized, cataloged, and analyzed in their relentless pursuit of the truth. Additionally, they sought assistance from the rental office, hoping to obtain valuable video surveillance footage to shed light on the criminal operations and potentially reveal additional individuals who had frequented the premises. Every lead was pursued with unwavering determination.

Simultaneously, the detectives employed a strategic approach at the Federal Detention Center to gather further information from the arrested individuals. Applying pressure during interviews, they sought to uncover valuable insights that could aid in unraveling the complete plot of the illicit organizations. Detective Jackie Ortiz noted with intrigue that some of the arrested individuals displayed limited English proficiency, indicating a common characteristic and suggesting they might be members of one organization. The fact that many medical supply company owners had resided in the country for a relatively short period intrigued the detectives, raising questions about the individuals' modus operandi and their overall objectives.

As the investigation unfolded, the detectives found themselves on the brink of uncovering the full extent of healthcare fraud activities in Miami. They understood the importance of connecting all the dots, piecing together the puzzle that would expose the syndicate's intricate web of deception and exploitation. The impending arraignment and subsequent legal proceedings presented a critical opportunity to gather more information and build a stronger case against the masterminds of the organization.

The task force remained vigilant, aware that their work was far from over. They knew dismantling the organization in Miami required unwavering commitment and a tireless pursuit of truth. With each passing day, the detectives grew closer to uncovering the inner workings of these organizations, determined to expose the full extent of their crimes and ensure that those responsible faced the consequences of their actions.

Detectives Julian Pratt and Jackie Ortiz leaned on their experience, intuition, and collective determination amidst uncertainty. These criminal organizations had remained elusive, but now the task force had them in their sights. As they delved deeper into the healthcare fraud and the criminal masterminds behind it, they were prepared to go to any lengths necessary to dismantle the criminal empire and restore justice to the healthcare system in South Florida.

As the arraignment unfolded, the tension in the courtroom was palpable. One by one, the defendants stood before the judge, each pleading not guilty. Their attorneys presented arguments, attempting to secure bonds and favorable outcomes for their clients.

Across the aisle, the U.S. Attorney, armed with a wealth of evidence and a steadfast determination to seek justice, fought vehemently to hold each individual without bond, pending a trial date. The prosecutor's unwavering stance reflected the gravity of the charges and the need to ensure the defendants' presence at their upcoming trials.

The back-and-forth between the defense and the prosecution was intense, with both sides making impassioned pleas to the judge. The defense argued for their client's rights, citing mitigating circumstances and the presumption of innocence, while the U.S. Attorney countered with the risk of flight and the potential danger to the community.

As the judge carefully considered the arguments, the defendants sat silently, their faces betraying a mix of apprehension and defiance. The courtroom was filled with the palpable tension of the legal battle unfolding, each side vying for the upper hand.

In the end, the judge's rulings reflected the delicate balance between upholding the rights of the accused and ensuring community safety. Some defendants were granted bonds, while others were remanded to custody—a decision that would shape the trajectory of the cases moving forward.

The U.S. Attorney, undeterred, continued to press forward, determined to bring these individuals to justice despite the challenges that lay ahead.

Detectives Julian and Jackie exchanged a knowing glance. They understood that the arraignment was just the beginning; the real battle lay ahead as they navigated treacherous waters, their every move scrutinized by those who sought to protect these organizations' secrets. But they were prepared. With strategy, resourcefulness, and unwavering determination, they were poised to expose the inner workings of the criminals and ensure justice prevailed.

As the dust settled from the arraignment, the task force dove deeper into the sea of evidence collected during the raids. Their mission remained clear: unravel the complete plot of these organizations and bring all those involved to justice. The countless documents, computers, and bank transactions provided a wealth of information, but it was like searching for a needle in a haystack.

The task force meticulously combed through each piece of evidence, with Julian Pratt linking the financial transactions to the individuals involved. They followed the money trail, piecing together a complex web of financial deceit that stretched far beyond what they had initially anticipated. It became apparent that the syndicate's operations were not limited to a few fraudulent medical supply companies but rather a sprawling network involving various actors across multiple industries.

Simultaneously, the task force conducted extensive interviews with the arrested individuals, applying pressure to elicit any additional information that could shed light on the inner circle's workings. They probed into their connections, roles within the organization, and any knowledge they possessed about the elusive figure who had thus far managed to evade capture. Each interview was a delicate dance, requiring a balance of coercion and empathy to extract the truth.

As Julian and Jackie delved deeper, they uncovered a troubling pattern. Many medical supply company owners, including those recently arrested, had resided in the country only briefly. This revelation heightened suspicions that one organization employed transient individuals, ensuring they could swiftly disappear should law enforcement get too close. It was a calculated strategy that had allowed the syndicate to remain one step ahead of their pursuers.

The evidence also pointed to the systematic exploitation of vulnerable individuals. The patients who had unknowingly become pawns in the syndicate's schemes recounted similar experiences. They had been contacted by telemarketers promising medical services and equipment, only to find that nothing was ever delivered. The syndicate had callously preyed on their trust and personal health information, pocketing the funds meant for their care.

This callous betrayal left the detectives even more determined to bring the syndicate to justice.

The task force connected the dots as days turned into weeks, creating a comprehensive picture of the criminal organization. The evidence led them through a labyrinth of false identities, shell companies, and illicit financial transactions. It became clear that this was not merely a case of isolated fraudulent activities but a sophisticated criminal enterprise with tentacles reaching into various industries.

With each breakthrough, the task force grew closer to identifying the elusive figure behind the syndicate's operations. They knew that unmasking this mastermind was crucial to dismantling the entire network. The investigation consumed their every waking moment, and their dedication remained unwavering in the face of mounting challenges.

The battle against these criminals was far from over.

The detectives were fully aware that their work had only just begun. They braced themselves for the arduous journey ahead, understanding that bringing down this sophisticated criminal organization would require persistence, ingenuity, and commitment.

As they pursued their mission, detectives Julian and Jackie Ortiz worked tirelessly, strategizing and analyzing each piece of information as it unfolded. They were resolute in exposing the Miami syndicate's inner workings and bringing all those involved to account for their crimes.

The investigation led them through a tangled web of deceit and corruption, with each new clue revealing deeper layers of criminal activities. Julian and Jackie remained undaunted, meticulously piecing together the puzzle, driven by an unwavering determination.

The road ahead was treacherous, with powerful adversaries conspiring to keep their illicit activities hidden. But the two detectives refused to be intimidated, pushing forward relentlessly, their assertive approach uncompromising in the face of threats and roadblocks.

As they closed in on their targets, Julian and Jackie demonstrated a commitment to their cause, using their keen intellect and investigative prowess to outsmart the syndicate's operatives at every turn. The stakes were high, but they never wavered, resolute in ensuring that those who had exploited the system faced the full consequences of their actions.

Chapter 7

UNRAVELING THE WEB

The memo from the U.S. Congress to the Florida U.S. Attorney's office sent shock-waves through the Miami task force investigating healthcare fraud in South Florida. As the magnitude of the criminal networks came to light, the detectives found themselves confronting a new level of complexity and danger in their pursuit of justice.

"The involvement of the Cuban government in facilitating the fraudsters adds a layer of intrigue," Julian said, his brow furrowed in concern.

Jackie leaned back in her chair, her expression grave. "The only plausible explanation I can see is that it's simply a matter of turning a blind eye to fugitives," she replied candidly.

The two seasoned detectives had seen their fair share of corruption, but this was a whole new level. The healthcare fraud scheme was vast, involving shell companies, offshore accounts, and with Miami as ground zero.

"They've got to be getting something in return," Julian murmured, his mind racing with possibilities. "What could the Cuban government possibly gain from protecting these criminals?" Jackie shook her head. "I don't know, but it's complicated."

The memo also reported an estimated annual loss of over $2 billion due to the fraud, and the urgency to act grew exponentially. The memo served as a stark reminder of the crime's magnitude and its devastating impact on taxpayers and the healthcare system in South Florida. It was a call to action, urging local authorities to step up their efforts and bring those responsible to justice.

The task force's determination was unwavering, but their hands were tied when the judge could not grant their request to revoke the bonds of suspects likely to escape. The absence of legal grounds for such a request underscored the complexity of the investigation. However, this setback only fueled the detectives' resolve to dig deeper and uncover the truth.

As the investigation reached a crucial juncture, the detectives began to confirm their hypothesis about the criminal network. The suspects had arrived in the country within the last two years, and their involvement in healthcare fraud and money laundering added another layer of complexity to the case. The illicit funds were concealed through various methods, making it challenging to trace their origins.

The task force intensified its surveillance on the individuals released on bail, keenly observing their interactions with other vehicles and documenting crucial evidence. The data on license plates and intelligence gathered from covert operations were key to unraveling the deceit the suspects had carefully woven.

Connecting the dots proved to be meticulous, requiring patience and precision. The task force sifted through mountains of data, searching for patterns and links that would lead them to the heart of the Miami syndicate's operations. Each piece of evidence was like a puzzle, waiting to be placed in its rightful spot.

As Julian Pratt and Jackie Ortiz delved deeper into their analysis, they made a stunning discovery. The information they had gathered not only implicated the suspects in the healthcare fraud scheme but also revealed links to members of a notorious crime organization based in Miami. The web expanded, exposing tendrils of corruption and deception that stretched far beyond their initial suspicions.

The task force understood the gravity of their findings and the need for utmost discretion. They knew that the crime organization would stop at nothing to protect its interests, and any misstep could jeopardize the investigation and put innocent lives at risk.

With the puzzle slowly taking shape, the task force coordinated their efforts, devising a plan to take down the criminal network once and for all. They knew the road ahead would be treacherous, but they were fueled by their unwavering commitment to justice and their desire to protect the vulnerable.

The evidence collected during the surveillance provided the much-needed breakthrough, linking the suspects to a notorious crime organization that had long evaded the grasp of law enforcement. The revelation sent shock-waves through the task force, confirming their worst fears: the syndicate's reach extended far beyond what they had initially imagined.

As detectives Julian and Jackie knew their next move would be critical. The stakes were higher than ever, and any misstep could let the syndicate slip through their fingers again. They gathered the team, their determination unwavering, and laid out the plan that would bring the criminals to justice.

The task force had to tread carefully, navigating a dangerous world of crime and corruption. Each team member understood the risks but was resolute in their commitment to protecting the innocent and restoring integrity to the healthcare system.

As the moon hung low in the night sky, the task force assembled at their designated meeting point. Julian Pratt knew this operation could be the turning point in their investigation. The suspects were cunning and resourceful, and the element of surprise would be their most potent weapon.

Julian Pratt and Jackie Ortiz had meticulously planned each raid, gathering intel on the suspects' routines and vulnerabilities. They knew that catching the criminals off guard was crucial to ensure a smooth and successful operation. The team split into groups, each assigned to a different target.

The first rays of dawn were still hours away when the task force silently approached the suspects' hideouts. Adrenaline coursed through their veins as they donned their tactical gear, ready to face whatever lay ahead. With a final nod of reassurance, they moved in.

At the first location, the suspect's residence was quiet, seemingly unaware of the impending storm. The team swiftly surrounded the building, taking strategic positions to cover every possible escape route. With a synchronized signal, they burst through the doors, shouting for everyone to get down.

Inside, the suspects were caught by surprise, their faces a mix of shock and fear. Their plans to evade justice had been foiled, and they now found themselves at the mercy of the law. Julian Pratt and Jackie Ortiz moved precisely, securing evidence and taking the suspects into custody.

Across the city, similar scenes played out at each location as the task force executed their well-coordinated plan. Each raid required split-second decision-making as suspects attempted to flee or hide evidence. But the detectives were relentless, their training and experience guiding them through the chaos.

With each successful raid, the task force grew more confident that they were dismantling the heart of the criminal network. But their work was far from over. The suspects were only pawns in a much larger game, and the true puppet masters were still out there, pulling the strings from the shadows.

As the detectives pieced together the puzzle, the shroud that had concealed the illicit operations began to lift. The web of deceit that had ensnared countless victims was now unraveling, revealing the true faces behind the healthcare fraud money laundering scheme.

As the sun rose, the detectives were shocked by the seized

documents. An accounting ledger filled with meticulous records of money owed and to be collected stood out. One name appeared repeatedly PMC. It was listed alongside substantial sums of money. The detectives exchanged a look, their suspicions piqued. It was more than obvious: this was a fine-tuned syndicate operation with a clear link between PMC and the money transactions.

Further down the list, another name caught their eye a restaurant in Little Havana. Raul's Cuban Cuisine.

Without hesitation, Julian and Jackie decided this restaurant would be the perfect starting point for their investigation and surveillance operation of the Miami Syndicate. They knew it would be easy prey, a soft target that likely had its fingers in all sorts of illicit activities.

They needed to follow the trail, unravel the mystery, and see where it led. Whatever was going on, it was bound to be big and potentially dangerous.

With the sun now high in the sky, the task force returned to their headquarters, ready to delve deeper into their investigation. The evidence they had seized during the raids was just the beginning—a glimpse into the complex network that had plagued South Florida.

Julian and the rest of the team knew their journey to bring down the Miami syndicate was far from over. The criminals they had apprehended were only a small part of a larger puzzle, and they were prepared to do whatever it took to expose the true masterminds behind the healthcare fraud and money laundering scheme.

As day turned into night, the task force continued their work in the shadows, their resolve unshaken. They knew that the fight for justice was arduous, but they were fueled by the knowledge that their efforts would protect countless innocent lives and restore integrity to the healthcare system in South Florida.

With each passing day, they drew closer to the truth, one step closer to bringing the Miami syndicate to its knees. As long as the darkness persisted, the task force would be there, ready to shine a light and unveil the secrets that had been hidden for far too long.

Chapter 8

A TWISTED ALLIANCE

As the investigation into the Miami syndicate intensified, the task force faced formidable adversaries and an internal struggle that tested the foundation of their unity. The revelation of a possible mole within their ranks sent shock-waves through the team, leaving them wary of each other and unsure whom they could trust. In times of crisis, their strength as a team was more critical than ever. Each detective knew they had to put aside their doubts and suspicions to focus on their common goal: dismantling the criminal network responsible for healthcare fraud in South Florida. They understood that the power of their collective effort far surpassed any individual contributions.

Julian Pratt and Jackie Ortiz, as the task force's lead detectives, took it upon themselves to bolster the team's spirits and reinforce the bond that held them together. They organized team-building exercises, encouraging open communication and fostering an environment of trust and support. They reminded their fellow detectives that they were all in this fight together, standing shoulder to shoulder against those who sought to exploit the vulnerable.

In their darkest moments, the task force leaned on each other for support. They shared their fears and vulnerabilities, acknowledging that feeling uncertain in the face of such betrayal was natural. But they also reminded one another of the countless lives they could save and the impact they could have on restoring integrity to the healthcare system.

Despite the shadows of deception looming overhead, the task force refused to succumb to fear or despair. They drew strength from knowing their cause was just and their dedication to the truth would prevail. They knew that adversity could tear them apart or strengthen their resolve, and they chose the latter.

During their surveillance at Raul's Cuban Cuisine, they noticed one of their own entering the establishment several times and speaking with the owner. Could this be a coincidence, or was something else happening behind closed doors?

The task force watched intently as Detective Scott Anderson, a seasoned detective in his late 50s with an average build, mustache, and beard, entered the restaurant for the third time that week. He appeared casual, even friendly, as he conversed with the owner and staff. Uncertainty gripped the team as they realized their most intimate secrets might have been compromised.

The investigation into healthcare fraud in South Florida was progressing smoothly, or so it seemed. Detective Julian Pratt had been working tirelessly to unravel the tangled web of illicit activities, leaving no stone unturned.

Meanwhile, the suspects' patterns and behaviors became a focal point in the investigation. The detectives noticed one common thread: the suspects frequented Raul's restaurant near downtown Miami.

Raul Dominguez, a Latin male in his early 60s, a bit overweight and seemingly unassuming, was known for hosting charity events attended by local politicians and law enforcement. The detectives kept a close eye on his restaurants, carefully monitoring their activities. It wasn't long before they spotted a well-dressed man in a sleek black Mercedes-Benz 500SL, constantly engaging with the owners and staff, almost as if he owned the place.

This sharply dressed individual immediately became a person of interest, a target of their investigation. They observed him making frequent visits, engaging in hushed conversations, and exchanging what appeared to be large sums of cash. The detectives couldn't help but wonder about his relationship with Raul, the restaurant owner.

As they dug deeper, a pattern emerged. The man in the Mercedes seemed to have an uncanny influence over the various establishments, almost as if he was calling the shots. The detectives suspected he might be involved in illicit activities, possibly using the restaurants as fronts for a larger criminal enterprise.

Working tirelessly to gather more evidence, Julian and Jackie delved deeper into the murky world of deceit and betrayal, hoping to catch any incriminating interactions. Late one evening, hidden in an unmarked van, they watched politicians and law enforcement personnel enter the restaurant for one of the charity events. Among them was Detective Anderson, sending a chill down Jackie's spine.

The sight prompted a tense exchange of glances between Jackie and Julian, who shared her apprehension. As the charity event progressed, they continued to observe, senses on high alert. The camaraderie between Detective Anderson and the restaurant owner seemed too rehearsed, too casual.

"We need to confront him," Jackie whispered, barely audible. Julian nodded, jaw clenched in determination. "We can't let this continue. Let's wait for the right moment."

As the night wore on, they bided their time, seeking the perfect opportunity to confront the suspected traitor without arousing suspicion. Their hearts pounded with anticipation and apprehension, knowing their actions could either vindicate their colleague or unveil a traitor.

Raul Dimnquez's involvement in charity events for politicians and law enforcement masked a darker truth: his ties to the criminal underworld ran deep. Now, with the seized documents revealing money transactions, questions arose about the PMC's motivations and its benefits to politicians.

The restaurant owner's establishment served as a haven for politicians and law enforcement personnel, fostering an environment where sensitive matters could be discussed freely.

One Miami task force agent found himself ensnared in this web of deceit. Mounting gambling debts left Detective Anderson vulnerable, and the restaurant owner saw an opportunity to exploit his precarious situation.

Trapped and desperate to erase his debts while preserving his reputation, Detective Anderson turned to the restaurant owner for financial relief. Unbeknownst to him, the cost of this bargain was his loyalty to the criminal network.

In exchange for financial assistance, he unwittingly

became a conduit of sensitive information, providing the syndicate with critical insights into the task force's investigation.

Chapter 9

DECEPTION UNRAVELED

The task force found themselves at a pivotal moment in their investigation of the Miami syndicate. Despite the shocking revelation of a mole within their ranks, their resolve to dismantle the criminal network remained steadfast.

Deep diving into the intricate paper trails and money flows, Detectives Julian and Jackie focused their efforts on several medical billing offices associated with the fraudulent medical supply companies. Their goal was to ascertain whether these offices were complicit in the scam or simply unaware of the syndicate's illicit activities.

Michael's sleek black Mercedes 500SL had become an emblem of power and influence within the Miami syndicate. Its presence at numerous crime scenes raised suspicions among the task force, casting Michael as a key suspect in their inquiry. Intensifying their surveillance efforts, the detectives were determined to catch him red-handed and bring him to justice.

His affiliation with Raul's restaurant, suspected to be a front for the syndicate, only added to the mounting evidence against him. Raul had cunningly positioned himself as a respected community figure, hosting charity events that attracted the attention of local politicians and law enforcement.

Michael's association with the restaurant provided him with a convenient guise to interact openly with politicians and law enforcement officials. Further investigation revealed that some of these interactions involved the exchange of sensitive information, deepening suspicions about Michael's motives.

Detective Julian was resolute in uncovering Michael's role within the Miami Syndicate. He assembled a skilled surveillance team reporting directly to him, tasked with meticulously documenting Michael's every visit to the restaurant.

The team would at times follow Michael, trailing him to meetings with the notorious Raul Dominguez and other suspicious characters. They observed them in secretive conversations, noting the palpable tension and suspicious glances that hinted at the high stakes involved.

As days stretched into weeks, the surveillance efforts intensified, revealing a discernible pattern in Michael's behavior. The restaurant emerged as a consistent meeting point, where Michael rendezvoused with associates and conducted cryptic phone calls in secluded corners. Detective Julian and his team were confident they were on the right track.

However, catching Michael in the act proved more challenging than anticipated. He was cautious and calculated, always evading direct involvement in illegal activities. The detectives had to be patient, waiting for the right moment to strike.

Their relentless efforts led them to observe Michael conversing with the manager of a currency exchange, raising further suspicions about money laundering. The task force moved swiftly, securing subpoenas from the state attorney to access the bank records of the currency exchange. They knew they were closing in on the Miami syndicate, and every piece of evidence was crucial.

In the world of covert operations, the line between right and wrong often blurs. Gabriel, the enigmatic leader of the Miami syndicate, found himself at such a crossroads, breaking his own cardinal rule to remain unseen.

Gabriel's mind raced as he picked up his phone and dialed the boat captain, Carlos Hernandez. The weight of their impending escape hung heavy in the air. He knew the risks involved, but there was no turning back now.

"Captain Hernandez, it's Gabriel," he said, his voice tense with anticipation.

"Gabriel, my friend," Captain Hernandez replied warmly. "What can I do for you?"

"I need to get the four individuals out of the country," Gabriel said in a hushed tone. "We can't afford to have them face trial here. We need to get them to Cuba."

Captain Hernandez hesitated momentarily before responding, "You know the risks we run without proper planning, Gabriel."

"I understand, Captain," Gabriel replied, determination shining in his eyes. "But we can't leave them here to face the consequences. Remember, this is what we do. We must do this for the syndicate and our survival."

Captain Hernandez sighed, realizing the gravity of the situation. "All right, I'll do it, although you've given me little time to prepare. We need to wait for the right moment. I won't risk the safety of my crew and the boat unless we have a clear path."

Gabriel nodded, his gratitude evident. "Thank you,

Captain. I'll keep you updated on the situation. Let me know when you're ready to go."

As the call ended, Gabriel felt a mix of relief and anxiety. He knew they were playing a dangerous game without future planning. This was a rush job, but it was a risk they had to take. The individuals were loose ends that needed to be tied up before they could threaten the syndicate's operations.

However, their plans faced an unexpected obstacle. Breaking news revealed that the Cuban government had arrested several rogue officials involved in a moneymaking scheme with Miami organizations. In response, Cuba declared they would not extradite their citizens, but any individuals caught with large amounts of money would face severe consequences.

The news of the Cuban government's arrests spread like wildfire through the streets of Miami, sending shock-waves of panic and uncertainty. Gabriel and Michael faced an unexpected obstacle that threatened to derail their plans.

"We can't travel freely to Cuba anymore," Michael muttered, frustration evident in his voice. "With the Cuban government cracking down on their officials, it's too risky."

Gabriel's brows furrowed as he paced back and forth, his mind racing for an alternative solution. "We can't let them face trial here either," he said firmly. "We need to get them out of the country before their court date."

Michael watched the situation unfold with a sense of urgency. The unforeseen turn of events demanded swift action to protect their interests. There was no room for hesitation or indecisiveness.

"I have an idea," Gabriel spoke up, his voice steady with determination. "We have connections in Chicago. We can arrange for new identities and safe passage for the individuals to a place where they can't be traced back to us."

Gabriel turned to Michael, a glimmer of hope in his eyes. "That might just work," he said. "We must act quickly before the authorities catch wind of our plan."

As the syndicate mobilized its resources, Gabriel contacted his friend in Chicago. "We have four individuals who need new identities and a way out of the country," Gabriel explained over an encrypted line. "Can you make it happen?"

His contact hesitated momentarily before replying, "It won't be easy, and it won't come cheap. But for the right price, I can arrange everything."

Money was not an issue for the syndicate. They had amassed considerable wealth through fraudulent schemes and were willing to pay whatever it took to ensure their survival.

As the hours passed, the syndicate's team worked tirelessly to finalize the arrangements. Fake passports, new identities, and discreet transportation were secured, all under the cover of darkness.

"The safe house will be ready in Mexico," the man added. "And I'll have my contacts on standby to provide protection and support."

A week before the court date, the four individuals gathered at a secluded location, their hearts pounding with fear and anticipation. Michael addressed them with a determined expression, assuring them of their safety.

"We've arranged everything," Michael said, his voice steady. "You'll be transported to a place where you can start fresh, away from the eyes of the authorities."

The individuals expressed their gratitude, knowing that their lives were now in the hands of the syndicate. They boarded a motor home that would take them to their new destination, far from the clutches of the law.

Relief washed over Michael as the vehicle drove off into the night. They had successfully navigated a treacherous path, ensuring the individuals would never testify against them.

However, they knew that their troubles were far from over.

The task force was still hot on their heels.

As the sun rose on the day of the court date, the syndicate's future hung in the balance. They knew the authorities would not give up their pursuit easily, and the battle for survival had just begun.

Gabriel and Michael stood side by side, their expressions resolute and unwavering. They knew their organization faced unprecedented challenges but were determined to rise above them.

"We'll weather this storm," Gabriel said, his voice filled with conviction. "We've overcome obstacles before and will do it again."

Michael nodded a steely glint in his eyes. "We're stronger together," he said. "And we won't let anyone bring us down."

The battle for the Miami syndicate's survival had reached a critical juncture. Betrayal, deception, and danger lurked around every corner, but the syndicate was determined to protect its empire at all costs. With their eyes on the future, Gabriel, Michael, and the PMC stood ready to face whatever challenges lay ahead.

Chapter 10

UNRAVELING THREADS OF DECEPTION

As the pressure mounted on Gabriel and Michael, they found themselves navigating a treacherous path, trying to keep their organization afloat amidst the chaos and the possibility that they had lost their Cuban safety net. With the Cuban government cracking down on their officials, they could no longer rely on the easy escape route they once had. They needed a new plan, and they needed it fast.

"We can't risk getting the individuals back to Cuba with their money now," Gabriel said, deeply concerned. "We need to find another way to get them out of the country without drawing attention."

Michael nodded, his mind already racing with possibilities. "We can't just walk into any airport; that's too risky," he said. "But we have other connections that might help us."

The two PMC founders huddled together, strategizing and brainstorming in the living room of Gabriel's apartment as they drank a bottle of Wood Reserve Bourbon. They discussed various options, weighing the risks and rewards of each.

As they deliberated, Gabriel and Michael considered the possibility of arranging private transportation for the individuals they needed to get out of the country. They knew they had to plan meticulously to avoid detection. They needed a method that would keep them off the grid and away from the prying eyes of law enforcement.

"We can't rely on commercial airlines or any public transportation," Gabriel said, his voice low and cautious. "We need something that won't raise suspicion and operates outside the regular channels."

Gabriel was getting desperate. The court date was looming, and he had to get his people out of the country fast. He had a stash of cash and four individuals who needed new identities. He dialed an old friend in Chicago and cut straight to the chase.

"Hey, man, I need a favor. Can you hook me up? I need a good connection in Mexico. I have four individuals who need to cross the border, and I also need fake papers and a safe house for them to stay."

"Give me 24 hours. I'll text you the details. Just be ready to move fast when the time comes," his friend responded.

Gabriel hung up the phone, his heart racing. He had to act fast and trust his friend to pull through. There was no turning back now.

The next day, Gabriel received the call he had been anticipating. His friend provided the details on where to meet the contact person. It was going to be near the border, in a small hotel, where he would obtain the fake documents needed to cross and move freely in Mexico.

"The safe house will be ready in Mexico," his friend assured him. "And I'll have my contacts on standby to provide protection and support."

Gabriel felt a mix of relief and anxiety. He knew they were playing a dangerous game, but it was a risk they had to take to ensure their survival.

"We trust you," Gabriel said, gratitude in his voice. "You're saving my ass with this operation."

The man laughed and replied with a firm, assuring voice, "Keep me posted. We'll always be here for you, just a phone call away. Take care, Gabriel. You're in good hands."

Gabriel and Michael exchanged a nod, and their resolve strengthened. They had come this far, and they would see the plan through to its end. With the man's assistance and the support of the Mexican organization, they had a fighting chance to execute their operation successfully.

Michael ordered one of the PMC members to start gathering the individuals. He explained to them that they would be leaving within hours and assured them that everything was going to be alright.

Gabriel knew the road ahead was treacherous, and they had to remain vigilant. But with their new ally by their side, they had a glimmer of hope that their operation would succeed.

Listen Michael we also have to structure our organization here at home we need to get back to basics, the weight of that thought hanging heavily in the air. The Possible loss of their Cuban connections loomed over them, forcing a reevaluation of their entire operation.

"We need to adapt," Gabriel said, his fingers drumming nervously on the counter-top. "The old ways might be our only option now."

Michael nodded, his eyes distant. "Recruiting locals. It's risky but necessary."

They began scouring their network, identifying potential candidates desperate enough to flee the country. Each name added to their list represented a life they would uproot, a future they would alter irrevocably.

As their plan took shape, the moral implications of their actions became impossible to ignore. They were offering an escape, yes, but at what cost? The promise of never returning to the United States, and living as fugitives in Cuba, weighed heavily on their consciences.

Meanwhile, the Miami Task-force huddled in their command center, their eyes fixed on the surveillance footage from various locations, especially Raul's restaurant and the currency exchange. Among the suspects they were closely monitoring, one name consistently rose to the top of the list: Michael. He was the central figure in their criminal profile, connecting all the pieces of the intricate puzzle they were trying to solve.

As they studied the evidence and analyzed the data, it became evident that Michael held a prominent position in the syndicate. He seemed to be the mastermind behind the operation, orchestrating the fraudulent activities meticulously. Detectives Julian and Jackie knew that taking him down would be crucial to dismantling the criminal network.

"He's the kingpin," one detective remarked, glancing at his colleagues, who nodded in agreement. "If we can get him, we'll have a better chance of uncovering the full extent of their operation."

They knew they had to be cautious. Michael was cunning, and any misstep could tip him off, sending the entire syndicate into a frenzy. The detectives strategized, contemplating their next move.

"He visits Raul's restaurant in Little Havana often," another detective said. "We need to keep a close eye on that place. It could be our key to getting to him."

Raul's restaurant had become a focal point in their investigation. It seemed more than just a place to dine; it was a hub where connections and secrets were exchanged. The detectives knew that if they could unravel the mysteries surrounding the restaurant, they might uncover the elusive web of criminal activities.

The surveillance intensified, with the detectives taking shifts to monitor the restaurant around the clock. They observed the patrons and staff interactions, searching for any signs of suspicious activity.

"He's there," one detective whispered, his eyes fixed on the live feed. "Michael just walked in."

They all leaned in, their focus sharpening as they watched Michael enter the restaurant. He moved confidently, exchanging greetings with the staff as he made his way to a corner booth.

"He's meeting with someone," the detective laughed. "The guy is cheating on his wife."

They watched intently as Michael greeted his companion, a short, average-bodied Latin woman with blond hair, 5'6", just as they had suspected. The detectives strained to hear their conversation, picking up bits and pieces through the bugs they had planted.

"This is a sensitive case," the lead detective warned. "We need to be careful not to jump to conclusions. For all we know, this could be a business meeting or a sexual encounter."

As Michael and the young woman finished their lunch, they stepped out into the parking lot, their hearts racing with anticipation. Without a moment's hesitation, they pulled each other close and locked lips in a passionate embrace, their bodies intertwined as the world around them faded away.

Breathless and gazing into each other's eyes with newfound intensity, they hurried to Michael's sleek Mercedes nearby, eager to continue their intimate encounter in privacy.

The engine roared to life as Michael and Betty peeled out of the restaurant parking lot. Their passionate kiss had ignited a fire within them, consumed by a desperate need for privacy.

Michael navigated the city streets urgently, while Betty's fingers traced patterns on his arms and chest. The air was thick with anticipation, the lingering scent of their passion hanging in the vehicle. Tension crackled between them—months of stolen glances and suppressed desires finally reaching a breaking point. Betty's perfume filled the air, intoxicating Michael with each breath. His grip tightened on the steering wheel with anticipation.

Their destination was unknown, but it hardly mattered. All that consumed their thoughts was the burning desire to be alone, to lose themselves in a tangle of limbs and whispered affection. The city buildings blurred past as they drove, their heartbeats racing. Within minutes, they had left the bustling streets behind, finding solace in a secluded hotel—a private sanctuary to finally give in to their passion, uninterrupted.

Betty's heart raced as she entered the hotel room, Michael close behind. The air crackled with electricity, months of unspoken desire finally given voice. Their eyes locked, a silent understanding passing between them. In an instant, they collided, lips meeting in a passionate frenzy. Hands roamed desperately, fingers tangling in hair and grasping at clothing.

As garments fell away, they savored each newly revealed inch of skin. Betty gasped as Michael's lips traced her collarbone, her fingers digging into his shoulders. They tumbled onto the bed, a tangle of limbs and breathless sighs. In the dim light, they explored each other with reverence and urgency. Betty arched beneath

Michael's touch, her body singing with pleasure. He worshipped her curves, committing every dip and valley to memory.

Their movements became more frantic, driven by primal need. Whispered endearments mixed with passionate cries as they lost themselves in sensation. The world outside ceased to exist; there was only this room, this moment, this connection. As they reached the pinnacle together, Betty cried out Michael's name. He held her close, their bodies trembling in the aftermath. They lay entwined, basking in the afterglow, neither willing to break the spell.

In the quiet that followed, reality began to seep back in. Betty traced patterns on Michael's chest, her mind racing. What would tomorrow bring? For now, she pushed those thoughts aside, determined to savor every remaining second of their stolen moment.

Betty's heart raced as she gazed into Michael's mesmerizing eyes, feeling the world around them melt away. The intensity of his gaze ignited a fire within her, and she found herself lost in the depths of his soul. Every fiber of her being yearned to stay in this perfect moment, to freeze time and bask in the electric connection they shared.

But reality crashed down upon her like a tidal wave. The weight of her wedding ring felt suddenly heavy on her finger, a stark reminder of the vows she had made to Randy Ramos. Guilt and desire warred within her as she reluctantly tore her eyes away from Michael's face.

"I... I have to go," Betty whispered, her voice trembling with emotion. "I need to get back to my husband."

With each step towards the bathroom, Betty felt as though she were walking through molasses. Her body screamed at her to turn back, to run into Michael's arms, and damn the consequences. But her sense of duty propelled her forward, even as her heart shattered with every inch of distance between them.

As she stepped into the shower, the hot water cascaded over her, mingling with the tears she could no longer hold back. Betty leaned against the cool tiles, her mind a whirlwind of conflicting emotions. The steam enveloped her, and she imagined it washing away the lingering traces of Michael's touch, the scent of his cologne, the memory of his lips so close to hers.

But even as she scrubbed her skin raw, Betty knew that no amount of water could cleanse her of the passion that now coursed through her veins. As they prepared to leave, she steeled herself for the inevitable heartache, knowing that a part of her would forever remain in that room, lost in the depths of his captivating gaze.

Michael and Betty exited the hotel room, their footsteps echoing in the empty hallway. The elevator ride was tense, neither daring to break the heavy silence between them. As they stepped into the parking lot, the breezy air did little to ease the burning intensity of their thoughts.

Michael gripped the steering wheel as he navigated the city streets back to the restaurant. The car's engine hummed, a stark contrast to the deafening silence between him and Betty. Her intoxicating perfume filled the air, each breath a bittersweet reminder of their stolen moments together.

He glanced at Betty, catching her eye for a brief, charged moment. The memory of her lips on his, her fingers trailing fire across his skin, threatened to overwhelm him. Michael forced himself to focus on the road, but his thoughts kept drifting back to their illicit rendezvous.

As they neared the parking lot where Betty's car waited, Michael's anxiety peaked. What if someone had seen them? What if word got back to her husband Randy? The potential consequences loomed large—not just for their business dealings, but for the lives they'd built.

Betty's hand suddenly covered his on the gearshift, sending a jolt through him. "Michael," she whispered, her voice husky with emotion. He turned to her, seeing the same conflict in her eyes that he felt in his heart.

They pulled into the restaurant parking lot, the car coming to a stop. For a long moment, neither moved. The air crackled with unresolved tension and lingering desire. Michael knew he should end it here, walk away, and never look back. But as Betty leaned in, her lips brushing his ear, he realized with both dread and excitement that this was far from over.

"Same time next week?" she breathed, sending shivers down his spine. Michael nodded, unable to resist the pull between them, even as he silently cursed his weakness. As Betty slipped out of the car and disappeared into a side street, Michael sat motionless, torn between regret and anticipation, knowing that their dangerous romance had only just begun.

But down deep inside Michael knew what he had done was wrong, a betrayal of trust on many levels. But in that moment, with Betty's lips on his and her hands roaming his body, all rational thought had fled. The forbidden nature of their encounter had only heightened the intensity, the raw passion igniting between them.

Now, as the adrenaline subsided, Michael was left with a deep sense of guilt. He had compromised his integrity and professional relationships for fleeting carnal pleasure. The weight of his actions threatened to crush him, the consequences looming large.

Yet, try as he might, Michael couldn't push away the

memory of Betty's touch, the way she had looked at him with eyes alight with wanton need. A part of him yearned to turn the car around, to seek her out again, to lose himself in her embrace once more. It was a temptation he knew he must resist, but the allure was powerful, a siren's call he feared he might not have the strength to ignore.

Chapter 11

THE PURSUIT AND PLANNING

Monday morning dawned with a sense of anticipation at the federal courthouse in downtown Miami. The task force had worked tirelessly to gather overwhelming evidence against the suspects involved in the Miami Syndicate. Detectives Julian Pratt and Jackie Ortiz, and the US attorney, Alice Harper, knew today would be a long day as they presented their case, unsealed their indictment against individuals, and sought arrest and search warrants, and bank seizures from the judge and grand jury.

Detective Jackie Ortiz stood before the judge, her voice clear and unwavering as she laid out the meticulously constructed case. Wiretaps, financial records, eyewitness accounts, and video surveillance it was an airtight presentation that left no room for doubt. The Miami Syndicate's intricate web of criminal activity had been unraveled, exposing the depth of their corruption.

As US Attorney Alice Harper presented the request for warrants, the judge's brow furrowed in concentration. This was a high-profile case with farreaching implications. One misstep could jeopardize the entire operation. But the evidence was irrefutable. With a resolute nod, the grand jury granted the warrants, authorizing the task force to move in and bring the suspects to justice.

Meanwhile, Gabriel and Sophia sat at a table near the bay, overlooking the Causeway from the quaint restaurant in Key Biscayne. The gentle breeze from the bay swept through, carrying the soothing scent of the ocean. It was a rare moment of tranquility for them amidst the chaos in Gabriel's life.

"Isn't this view just breathtaking?" Sophia said, her eyes sparkling with joy as she gazed at the Miami skyline.

Gabriel smiled, his normally guarded expression softening in the presence of Sophia's infectious happiness. "It certainly is," he replied, sipping his coffee. "I can't believe we haven't done this in a long time."

Sophia laughed lightly, reaching across the table to

place her hand on his. Gabriel's heart skipped a beat at her touch. He opened up in ways he never thought possible with Sophia. She had a way of making him feel at ease, melting the icy walls around his heart.

Gabriel felt a sense of peace wash over him as they chatted and savored their breakfast. For once, he could put aside the burdens of his criminal organization and enjoy a moment of normalcy. It was as if the world around them had faded away, leaving only the two wrapped in their shield of happiness.

"I have to admit, I never thought I'd find myself in a situation like this," Gabriel confessed, his gaze locking with Sophia's.

She smiled warmly, her eyes filled with understanding. "Life has a way of surprising us, doesn't it? But I'm glad we found each other, Gabriel."

He reached across the table to caress her cheek gently. "So am I," he murmured, his voice barely above a whisper.

Their fingers intertwined, and they sat in comfortable silence, lost in each other's eyes. It was a rare moment of vulnerability for Gabriel, a side of him that few had ever seen. But with Sophia, he felt safe, accepted, and loved.

As they finished their breakfast, Gabriel felt a sense of hope hope for a future where he could leave behind his criminal life and embrace a new beginning with Sophia by his side.

"Let's take a walk along the bay," he suggested, a hint of excitement in his voice.

Sophia nodded eagerly, her eyes shining. They paid the bill and made their way toward the bay, the sun embracing them warmly. Hand in hand, they strolled along the water's edge, the waves lapping gently against the shore.

The salty breeze ruffled their hair as they admired the breathtaking view. Sophia felt a sense of wonder, captivated by the serene beauty of the bay.

"Isn't this just perfect?" she said, squeezing his hand.

He smiled, his gaze locked with hers. "It is. I'm so glad we decided to come out here."

They continued their stroll, content to enjoy each other's company and the tranquil surroundings. Sophia knew she wouldn't want to be anywhere else.

As they walked hand in hand, Gabriel felt a glimmer of hope for a future filled with love, redemption, and a new beginning. The road ahead was uncertain, but he knew anything was possible with Sophia by his side. Little did he know what awaited at the end of this bright and happy tunnel.

As Gabriel continued his daily activities, checking in with his point of contact within the PMC, the detectives maintained their stakeout on the suspects, meticulously following their every move to ensure they remained unaware of the impending take-down.

A sense of urgency filled the task force headquarters as the team strategized their plan. They decided to target the rogue Detective Anderson and Raul, the restaurant owner, a couple of days before the main operation. These individuals seemed the weakest links and could potentially be persuaded to turn government witnesses against the Miami Syndicate.

Months of planning and intelligence gathering led to this moment. The team was well-trained and highly disciplined, working seamlessly to secure the locations simultaneously, leaving no chance for the suspects to react or mount a defense.

As the operation unfolded, the sound of splintering wood and shouted commands filled the air. Suspects were forced to the ground and restrained, offering little resistance in the overwhelming show of force. The tactical unit moved with unwavering purpose, driven by dismantling this dangerous criminal network.

In the aftermath, the suspects were transported to Federal facilities in Miami, where they would be interrogated and processed. The team knew this was just the beginning they needed to question those detained to get full clarity on Michael Cruz's involvement and determine if he needed to be indicted as well and face the law's full extent. But at this moment, the take-down had been a success.

And now it was the moment of truth. Detective Jackie Ortiz took a deep breath as she entered the interrogation room where the rogue Detective Anderson sat, his hands cuffed on the table in front of him. She had known and trusted Anderson for years as a partner on the Miami task force, and the thought of him betraying their team was almost too much to bear.

"Anderson," she said steadily as she sat across from him. "Why? Why would you do this?"

Anderson avoided her gaze, staring down at the table. "I...I don't know, Jackie. It just happened so fast. One minute I was doing my job, the next..." He trailed off, shaking his head.

"The next what?" Jackie pressed. "The next you were in bed with the enemy? Leaking information? Putting all of our lives at risk?" Her voice rose with each word, the hurt and anger she felt seeping through.

Anderson flinched, finally meeting her eyes. "I never meant for anyone to get hurt. I just...I got greedy, I got myself into debt, gambling issues. I should have asked you guys for help. But the role of money offered to me seemed to be, at the time, a simple way out to pay back my debt. It was too good to pass up. I thought I could handle it, that I could keep it all under control."

Jackie scoffed. "Well, you were wrong. And now you've betrayed everything we've worked for everything we believe in." She leaned forward, her eyes narrowing. "Do you have any idea what kind of damage you've done?"

Anderson opened his mouth to respond, but no words came out. He knew there was no excuse, no justification for his actions.

He had made a terrible mistake, and now he would have to face the consequences.

Jackie shook her head, disappointment is evident on her face. "I trusted you, Anderson. We all did. And you threw that away for what? A few bucks?" She stood up, turning to leave. "I hope it was worth it. By the way, I have a question. What do you know about Michael Cruz? Just a simple yes or no do you know anything?"

Anderson responded, "I've seen him around. I've never had a conversation with him. Just a hi and bye. I do not know anything about what he does or his personal life."

As the door clicked shut behind her, Anderson felt the weight of his betrayal crushing him. He had let down not just his partner, but his entire team his family. And there was no going back.

Meanwhile, Detective Julian Pratt entered another

interrogation room, his eyes narrowing as he studied Raul, the restaurant owner, sitting before him, hands cuffed and resting on his legs.

"All right, let's cut to the chase," Julian said bluntly. "We've got you. We know you were involved, so you might as well start talking."

Raul stared back at Julian, his expression defiant. "I'm not saying a word until my attorney gets here."

Julian leaned forward, palms flat on the table. "Look, this would go a lot easier for you if you cooperated. We've got evidence. You're only making it worse for yourself by clamming up. What can you tell me about Michael Cruz?"

But Raul remained silent, his lips pressed into a thin line.

Frustration flickered across Julian's face. "Fine. Have it your way." He pushed himself up and headed for the door. "Your lawyer better get here quick. Because you are not going anywhere you're looking at a lot of time behind bars."

The door slammed shut, leaving Raul alone with his thoughts, the cuffs biting into his wrists. He knew he was in deep trouble, but he also knew his rights. No way was he going to incriminate himself, not without his attorney present. He just had to hold out a little longer.

The next day, Detectives Julian Pratt and six more

agents arrived at the medical billing office of Randy and Nancy Ramos, placing them both under arrest along with some staff members. The Ramos couple had been running an elaborate healthcare and insurance fraud scheme for years, associated with the Miami syndicate.

As Randy and Nancy Ramos were led into separate interrogation rooms, Detectives Julian and Jackie exchanged a knowing glance. They knew this was going to be a challenging case, but they were determined to get to the truth.

Entering the room, Detective Julian faced the stone-faced Randy, who sat silently, arms crossed, refusing to cooperate. "Mr. Ramos, we have a lot of evidence that points to you and your wife running a fraudulent medical billing scheme. You're in a lot of trouble here, so I'd advise you to start talking. First, I want to help you what do you know about Michael Cruz? His car has been seen parked at your office more than once."

Randy remained silent, his expression unwavering. "I'm not saying anything without my lawyer present."

Next door, Detective Jackie Ortiz approached the equally defiant Nancy. "Mrs. Ramos, we know you and your husband have been doing some shady stuff. You're looking at some serious jail time if you don't start cooperating. Start by telling me what is your relationship with Michael Cruz?"

Nancy shook her head defiantly. "I want my attorney. I'm not admitting to anything."

Randy Ramos's lawyer was approached by Detective Jackie Ortiz just as they were about to visit Randy at the Federal Detention Center. Jackie had a serious look on her face as she requested a private word with the lawyer.

"Look, I know this case is tough for your client," Jackie began candidly. "But I think I might be able to help your client if he's willing to cooperate with me."

The lawyer eyed her skeptically. "What kind of information are you talking about?"

"Information about Michael Cruz," Jackie replied. "Let's take a walk and see what you have."

The interrogation room was tense as Randy sat across the table from Jackie. Jackie slid a file folder toward Randy.

"I've got some information here you need to see," Jackie said bluntly. "It's going to change everything."

After a tense moment, Randy nodded. "Alright, let's see what you've got."

Randy opened the file, revealing the damning photographs. His eyes narrowed as he pored over the images his wife Nancy and Michael Cruz, caught amid their passionate affair, entering hotel rooms, dining at restaurants. The visual proof was irrefutable. he looked up, his gaze hardening. "What do you want to know?" There was a new resolve in his voice, a willingness to confront the ugly truth head-on. The betrayal stung, but he was ready to face it, to uncover the full extent of his wife's deception. Whatever Jackie had to offer, Randy would listen he needed to know the whole story, no matter how painful.

As the hours passed, the news of the arrests could not be suppressed. The Miami Syndicate's reach was far and wide, and they had eyes and ears in every corner of Miami. Michael received a phone call, updating him on the events that had taken place earlier that morning.

He gripped the steering wheel tightly as he drove through the city streets, his hands turning white. The news he received sent a chill down his spine – Raul, Nancy, her husband, and others were in federal custody. He knew at that moment he had to get to a safe house, to warn Gabriel and the rest of the PMC.

Michael exhibited a touch more finesse. He patiently bided his time, selecting the cover of nightfall as his opportune moment. He precisely established contact with an associate from the Miami syndicate, ensuring utmost secrecy. Their rendezvous point was a dimly lit parking garage without prying surveillance eyes. Michael quickly pocketed the new cell phone, his fingers deftly concealing the exchange. He knew the importance of this transaction a fresh clone cellular phone to throw off any possible pursuit.

As dawn broke a couple of days later, law enforcement descended upon Michael's residence, only to discover he was gone only his wife and kid remained. Michael had a head start on them. He had cunningly slipped through their fingers.

Michael's wife, once oblivious to his true nature, now found herself caught in the cross-hairs of the law, her pleas of ignorance falling on deaf ears. With each passing hour, the net tightened around Michael's whereabouts. Detectives Julian and Jackie, determined to bring him to justice, scoured the city, leaving no stone unturned. But Michael, a master of evasion, had planned his escape meticulously, anticipating their every move.

Meanwhile, Michael remained one step ahead, his freedom a bitter victory over the system he had so skillfully manipulated. The thought of his family, especially his kids' uncertain future, weighed heavily on his mind, but his sense of self-preservation eclipsed all else. He knew that the price of his freedom would be high, but he was willing to pay it, no matter the cost.

Michael made a call, and Gabriel's voice crackled through the line in hushed tones, directing Michael to a secure sanctuary in Naples, Florida. A journey of around 100 miles westward from Miami, this safe house was perched along the tranquil shores of the West Coast.

Gabriel and Michael met up in Naples, Florida. Gabriel was surprised. "Why are they looking for you, Michael?" he asked. "Do you have any idea why? I can't understand even if there are people arrested, we have filters in place to avoid being singled out in any criminal case. I don't understand what's going on."

Michael replied, "I just know that my house was raided. This meeting was ordained, and the choreography of survival unfolded."

"All right, Michael, listen up," Gabriel said, his voice low and serious. "We don't have much time, so I'm going to give it to you straight. This is the best-case scenario you've got. Let's think out of the box what do we do with our resources?"

Michael responded, "You're not suggesting that I flee to Cuba?"

"Have you lost your mind? Did you forget? There were a lot of government officials arrested in Cuba because of criminal ties to Miami. We haven't spoken to our government friend in a long time. We don't know if he's in jail or what his whereabouts are. And for all we know, we may have been implicated. That's one place I do not want to be a part of."

Gabriel, acutely aware of the simmering urgency, comprehended the gravity of their situation. Both men shared the common imperative: to traverse the borders into Mexico, where the heat had yet to reach its scorching zenith.

The prosecutors vehemently opposed granting bail to any arrested individuals at the courthouse, considering them all high-flight risks. The evidence presented was overwhelming, and the case against the defendants seemed rock-solid.

As the proceedings unfolded, Gabriel, the elusive figure of the Miami Syndicate, remained a ghost, untouched by the law enforcement dragnet. The detectives knew that Michael was the key player, based on the information provided by his now co-defendant, Randy Ramos. This was a case about betrayal, but Michael remained a wanted man, stubbornly defiant in the face of the mounting evidence.

The detectives had hoped that more of the arrested individuals might flip and provide the crucial information they needed to bring Michael Cruz down. But so far, the loyalties of all the Syndicate members had proven to be stronger than the threat of prosecution.

But Michael remained one step ahead, disappearing into the night. Detective Jackie Ortiz knew it was only a matter of time before he resurfaced, and she was determined to be there waiting for him. She vowed to hunt down the elusive Syndicate member and bring him to justice, no matter the cost.

Once again, Gabriel extended his request through the Chicago connection, this time with a heightened sense of urgency. He needed a discreet safe house nestled within Cancun, as well as a set of fake documents a driver's license and other identification.

Without hesitation, his Chicago associates contacted their network in Cancun. This network could provide the kind of secure, off-the-grid accommodations Gabriel required. Within hours, a safe house had been secured an unassuming townhouse tucked away in a quiet residential neighborhood, far from prying eyes.

In the intricate web of Miami's legal battles, Gabriel finds himself at a crossroads. The realization that he might lose his trusted friend and ally, Michael, weighs heavily on him. As they strategize together, Gabriel knows that he must consider the possibility of appointing a temporary replacement. This decision is not taken lightly, as the outcome of Michel Cruz's case could pivot on the strength and wisdom of this interim figure. Gabriel's choice will be a testament to his leadership and foresight in navigating the treacherous waters of Miami's justice system.

Gabriel's eyes lock onto Michael, his gaze intense and unwavering. The air between them crackles with unspoken tension as Gabriel finally breaks the silence.

"Call Raphael," Gabriel commands, his voice low and resolute. "I need to meet him face to face."

Michael's brow furrows, concern etching deep lines across his forehead. "Gabriel, are you sure that's wise? Meeting Raphael now could—"

"We don't know what the outcome of all this is going to be," Gabriel interrupts, his words sharp and decisive. "We need to set our priorities in place."

Gabriel's eyes blaze with determination as he continues, "And for right now, we need to make sure that Raphael Santos is up to speed on how to run the operation correctly, with us not being hand-son."

Michael hesitates, weighing the gravity of Gabriel's words. The passion in Gabriel's voice is palpable, infusing every syllable with urgency and conviction.

"This isn't just about us anymore," Gabriel presses on, his voice rising with emotion. "It's about the future of the Miami Syndicate that we've built. The PMC needs to stay intact, even without us if need be. We've sworn to protect it.

Gabriel's fists clench at his sides, his entire body taut with resolve. "Raphael needs to be prepared. He needs to understand the weight of what's coming."

Michael finally grasps the full implications of Gabriel's decision. The air around them seems to pulse with the intensity of the moment.

"Make the call," Gabriel commands once more, his voice softening but losing none of its passion. "It's time Raphael stepped into his destiny. And it's time we faced ours."

As Michael reaches for his cloned cellular phone, the weight of their impending meeting with Raphael hangs heavy in the air— a pivotal moment that could change the course of Michael's life.

Michael's hand reaches for the cloned cellular phone, its sleek surface cool against his clammy palm. He meets Gabriel's intense look, seeing the fire of determination burning in his partner's eyes.

The air crackles with tension, thick with the weight of their decision.

As Michael dials, memories flood his mind—years of careful planning, countless risks taken, and sacrifices made. The Miami Syndicate has been their passion, their purpose. But now, everything hangs in the balance.

The phone rings once, twice, three times. Michael's heart pounds in his chest, each beat a reminder of what's at stake. Finally, a voice answers.

"Raphael," Michael says, his voice steady despite the turmoil within. "It's time. We need to meet."

There's a pause on the other end. Then, Raphael's voice, low and cautious: "Where?"

Michael relays the location in Naples, Florida, tonight, his words charged with urgency. As he ends the call, he turns to Gabriel, seeing a mix of fear and excitement mirrored in his partner's face.

As the hours pass, they move swiftly, gathering their thoughts for the meeting. The city blurs past as they drive, the streetlights a stark contrast to the darkness of their mission. Michael's mind races, envisioning the potential outcomes—success, failure, betrayal, or something entirely unexpected.

As they arrive at the meeting point in downtown Naples, Florida, Michael feels the weight of destiny pressing down on him. Gabriel squeezes his shoulder, a gesture of solidarity and strength.

They step out of the car, the cool night air a sharp reminder of the reality of their situation. In the distance, they see a figure approaching—Raphael Santos, walking toward his destiny and towards the moment that will define their future within the Miami Syndicate.

Michael takes a deep breath, steeling himself for what's to come. Whatever happens next, there's no turning back. The die is cast, and the future of the Miami Syndicate—and their lives—will hang on Raphael Santos's shoulders.

Gabriel's eyes narrow as he extends his hand to Raphael, a knowing smirk playing at the corners of his mouth. "A pleasure to meet you, Raphael," he says, his look penetrating and intense. "I've heard... a lot."

Raphael's grip is firm, his eyes looking with a mixture of pride and caution. The air between them crackles with unspoken understanding.

Michael watches the exchange, a hint of satisfaction in his stance. He clears his throat, "Raphael here has been invaluable to our organization. His knowledge of our... lifestyle... is unparalleled."

Gabriel's smirk widens. "Is that so?" Gabriel never breaks eye contact with Raphael. "Well, the Miami Syndicate doesn't keep just anyone around for long. You must be quite the asset."

Raphael's chest swells slightly at the praise. "I've dedicated myself to the cause," he replies, his voice low and filled with conviction. "This isn't just business. It's a thrill I never liked living a simple life I need the excitement.

The three men stand in a triangle of power, the small town of Naples glittering behind them.

Gabriel finally releases Raphael's hand, but the intensity remains. "I look forward to seeing your expertise in action, Raphael. The family values loyalty above all else. And talent... well, talent like yours doesn't go unnoticed."

Michael claps both men on the shoulders. "Gentlemen,

I believe this is the beginning of a very fruitful partnership. Shall we discuss the upcoming operation?"

"I want to thank you for coming," Gabriel says, his voice low. "We need to talk about Michael's situation."

Raphael nods, tension evident in his shoulders. "How bad is it?"

"Bad enough. The detectives raided his house. Depending on how it plays out, we might need to restructure things." Gabriel leans forward, his eyes intense. "That's where you come in."

Raphael's heart races. "What do you need me to do?"

"I'm going to be out of the picture for a couple of weeks, maybe a month. Laying low. You'll be taking on more responsibility. Think you can handle it?"

Raphael hesitates, then nods firmly. "I'm ready."

Gabriel slides a cloned cellular phone across the table. "Use this only for my calls, no one else. I'll be in touch. Raphael?" He pauses, his look hardening. "Don't screw this up."

"As Raphael started his drive back to Miami, the weight of his new responsibility settles on his shoulders. He knows the risks, but also the potential rewards. Whatever happens with Michael, things are about to change."

Early Monday morning in Miami, Raphael Santos starts to vet potential attorneys. He discovers the U.S. Attorney's office, raising the stakes further. Gabriel periodically checks in, emphasizing the importance of finding a skilled lawyer who can navigate the intricacies of Raul Dominguez's case. Gabriel Cortez sees things; if he pays for the lawyer, he has certain inside knowledge of the case. Any possible snitching of anyone leaking information the law enforcement.

As the days passed after the meeting in Naples Florida, Gabriel and Michael crossed the border, and as he settled into a safe house in Mexico, Gabriel felt a mixture of relief and unease. However, he also recognized the importance of buying time and avoiding capture. Gabriel couldn't shake the worry gnawing at him. He knew he had to call Sophia, but he also knew he couldn't reveal the truth of his situation. The less she knew, the safer she would be.

Gabriel had his trusted syndicate members take a clone cellular phone that was not linked to either of them. He knew that communication was crucial, but they couldn't risk being traced back to him by law enforcement.

He picked up his hot cellular and dialed her number, his heart racing as he waited for her to answer. When her voice came through the line, he felt relief and guilt. Sophia had been worried sick about him, and he hated keeping her in the dark about his plans.

"Sophia," he said, his voice soft yet urgent. "It's me."

There was a moment of silence on the other end before she responded, her voice laced with concern. "Gabriel, where are you? What's going on? Why did you have someone else give me this cellular and inform me to break it and throw it away in five days?"

He took a deep breath, trying to find the right words. "I had to take precautions," he explained. "Michael was being watched, and I can't risk anyone tracking our communication."

"I don't understand," Sophia replied, her worry evident. "What's going on, Gabriel? Why are you hiding?"

He hesitated momentarily, trying to decide how much he could tell her without putting her in danger. "A lot is happening, Sophia," he said finally. "I can't explain everything right now, but I need you to trust me."

"I do trust you, Gabriel," she said softly. "But I can't help but worry. I've seen the news on TV and know what they're saying about Michael and the people associated with him."

Gabriel's heart sank. He hated that his actions were causing her pain, but he couldn't back down now. "I promise you, Sophia, I'm doing everything I can to protect you and our future," he said earnestly. "I need you to stay safe and stay away from any attention. If anyone asks, you know nothing."

"I'll do whatever you ask, Gabriel," she said, her voice filled with determination. "But please, promise me you'll return to me."

He closed his eyes, feeling the weight of his promise. "I will come back," he said firmly. "I'll make sure of it."

They talked for a little longer, Gabriel assuring her he was doing what needed to be done to ensure their safety. "I know it's hard not knowing everything," he said, his voice tender. "But I need you to trust me, Sophia. I'll explain everything when I can."

She took a shaky breath. "Okay, Gabriel," she said, her voice wavering but filled with love and support. "I trust you. Just promise me you'll be careful."

"I promise," he said, his voice filled with determination. "I'll do whatever it takes to protect you and our future."

As they said their goodbyes, Gabriel felt a mix of emotions. He hated keeping Sophia in the dark but knew it was the only way to keep her safe. He vowed to do whatever it took to ensure their future together, even if it meant facing the dangerous and uncertain path ahead.

Gabriel stared at his cellular phone for a long time, feeling the weight of his choices. He knew he had to protect Sophia, even if it meant keeping her in the dark.

As the days turned into weeks, Julian and Jackie

continued to build their case against the Miami syndicate. They tirelessly interviewed witnesses, analyzed phone records, and gathered every piece of evidence they could find. The pressure on the arrested individuals was mounting, and some started considering cooperating with the authorities in exchange for leniency.

Gabriel remained vigilant inside the safe house in Cancun, knowing that the syndicate's survival depended on his leadership. He kept in touch with one trusted syndicate member, offering him guidance and assurance that they would emerge stronger from this setback.

The court case progressed in Miami, and the evidence against the syndicate grew stronger daily. The detectives were determined to bring all those involved to justice, including the elusive mastermind.

Chapter 12

CELEBRATIONS AND SHADES OF GABRIEL

Meanwhile, in Miami, Raul Dominguez's Attorney requested a meeting with U.S. Attorney Alice Harper to discuss his case. The meeting was set to take place in the U.S. Attorney's Office, across the street from the courthouse.

On the day of the meeting, Raul Dominguez's attorney, the sharp-tongued litigator Mr. Green, strode across the street from the courthouse to the U.S. Attorney's office. He was ushered into Alice Harper's spacious, impersonal workspace, the kind that screamed authority.

Mr. Green launched into the details of Raul's case. "All right, let's get to the point. The Government hit my client with a laundry list of charges racketeering, money laundering, fraud, counter surveillance, the whole nine yards. Now, I've gone through the discovery, and I gotta say, the evidence is looking pretty weak."

Alice listened impassively, "Your client was caught red-handed, Mr. Green. We have him on tape, eyewitness accounts, and the paper trail is very damaging."

"Oh, I'm sure it looks that way to you," Mr. Green leaned back in his chair, affecting an air of casual confidence. "But I'm telling you, there's more to this story. Raul's no angel, but he's not the mastermind you're making him out to be. This whole thing reeks of a setup."

The back-and-forth continued, with Mr. Green poking holes in the prosecution's case and Alice stubbornly defending it. Both were seasoned veterans, unwilling to concede an inch. The air crackled with tension as they traded barbs and legal arguments.

Finally, Alice sighed. "Look, I get that you're going to bat for your client, and I'm aware he is not the mastermind. But the facts are the facts. If you've got something substantial to bring to the table, I'm willing to listen. Otherwise, I'm afraid this conversation is over, and I will see you in court."

The air was tense as the lawyer and prosecutor sat across the table from one another. Both knew this was a critical moment a chance to find some middle ground before the trial that was a month away.

Mr. Green spoke first, "OK, let's compromise. Last week, I suggested to my client to testify on his co-defendants, something that he objects to very highly. If your office cuts Raul a sweet deal, I could persuade him. But something else that's not negotiable, we need to keep him off the record as a government witness. In return, you will give Raul a minimal sentence in a federal detention camp."

Alice Harper sighed. "Alright, how about this we keep Raul off the record. He debriefs us on the Syndicate's whole operation, no holding back, or the deal is off. We'll give him a cushy minimum security camp afterward. Beats spending fifteen to twenty behind bars, doesn't it?"

"Alright, I'll go back and talk to him. But you gotta give me something in return," the lawyer said, leaning forward. "I need a guarantee that you'll keep his identity under wraps."

Alice Harper pursed her lips, thinking it over. After a moment, she extended her hand. "Deal. You get him to testify, and I'll make sure he doesn't end up having to do the full-time that he deserves. But this is a onetime offer, Mr. Green. You better make it count."

Mr. Green felt the weight of the decision settles on his shoulders. Time to convince Raul to betray everything he knew. It wasn't going to be easy, but sometimes in these illicit businesses, you had to make tough choices.

A few days later, I sat down with Raul to discuss the details. I wanted to be completely candid about the situation, with no sugarcoating or false hopes. "Listen, Raul, I need you to testify," his jaw clenched. "No way in hell am I testifying against the Miami Syndicate. We're family." Raul leaned forward, eyes narrowed.

"Look, Raul, I get it. But you're facing 15 to 25 years if you don't cooperate. We can make this a lot easier on you."

Raul scoffed. "Easier? You want me to betray the only people who've ever had my back." He shook his head. "I'd rather rot in prison than snitch."

"Listen, Raul, it's a simple deal, hear me out. Testify against the Miami Syndicate. The best part is that no one will find out you testified. That's the only way this will work," Mr. Green said sternly. Raul knew there was no going back once he signed on the dotted line. My old life would cease to exist; I'd be entrusting my future to the government what a lifestyle change.

"One more thing, at my meeting with the U.S. Attorney, she kind of whispered in secrecy. She told me to tell you that they had found a weak spot, a way to get to you where it hurt the most." Raul tried to keep his composure, but the worry had shown on his face. "They're saying they have incriminating evidence against your wife?"

I knew then that I was trapped. They had me over a barrel, and there was nothing I could do. My wife's freedom, her future, it was all hanging by a thread.

Raul Dominguez swallowed hard, his mouth suddenly dry. "What do you want me to do? I will cooperate, but I have no choice. Who will take care of my kids if my wife gets implicated in this case?" Give me a day, and I will testify what I know.

Detective Julian Prat sighed heavily; weariness evident in his eyes as he spoke to his colleague. "It's been a long and hard-fought battle, but we've made significant progress. Raul's legal counsel strongly advises him to consider a guilty plea and an agreement to forfeit properties and funds. The case presents an abundance of compelling evidence against him, particularly concerning charges of bribery, extortion, counter-surveillance on law enforcement, and the obstruction of criminal investigations within the Miami syndicate."

"In a parallel development, additional individuals implicated in the case, including a married couple, Nancy pursued a plea bargain due to her involvement in a healthcare fraud scheme. Randy is getting a sweet deal for his cooperation in the case. Their medical billing company played a pivotal role in orchestrating a substantial volume of falsified claims amounting to over $60 million, which were submitted to the healthcare system as part of their association with the syndicate. As a result, they are confronting the prospect of facing sentences ranging from nine to fifteen years. Furthermore, certain lower-level employees of the billing company, who played comparatively minor roles in the illicit operation, may be subject to imprisonment periods ranging from three to five years."

His fellow detective nodded, acknowledging the magnitude of the victory. "At least justice is finally catching up with them," he said solemnly.

"Yeah," the detective replied, "but it's not over yet. We still have Michael out there and don't even know where he is. He's like a ghost, slipping through our fingers whenever we get close."

The task force had been chasing Michael for months, trying to pin down the elusive Miami Syndicate mastermind. Every time they thought they had a lead, he vanished without a trace.

The detectives glanced around the room, where their fellow task force members celebrated the successful takedown of many syndicate members. Despite the joyous atmosphere, a cloud of uncertainty loomed over them. Michael's absence cast a long shadow, a reminder that their mission was far from complete.

As they sipped their drinks during the toast given by

the U.S. Attorney Alice, the name "Michael" escaped the lips of the speaker. The mention was unintentional but not unnoticed. The detective exchanged a knowing glance with his partner, understanding the weight of that name in their investigation.

"We've made a significant dent in the syndicate, and that's no small feat," the U.S. Attorney's voice boomed, commanding the attention of everyone in the room. "But we can't forget that the mastermind behind it all, Michael, is still at large. Rest assured; we will not rest until he is brought to justice."

The promise elicited a chorus of resolute nods and determined expressions from the task force members. They were a team forged in the crucible of this complex investigation, united by a shared goal: to dismantle the Miami syndicate and bring all its members to justice.

Time passed, and Gabriel felt it was safe to reach out to his trusted member Raphael of the Miami syndicate. He summoned a couple of the most trusted members for a clandestine meeting in Cancun to discuss his new plan for the organization. The syndicate members, still wary of the recent crackdown, gathered in Orlando and boarded their planes, far from the city of Miami.

In the dark underworld of the Miami Syndicate, trust was a currency more precious than gold. Gabriel knew this all too well, and his decision to reach out to Raphael

Santos, the enigmatic figure known as El Chino, was not one he took lightly. Gabriel turned to Michael Cruz and instructed him to make the call. This would be the second time Gabriel would meet Raphael Santos (El Chino) face-to-face, a prospect that filled him with equal parts anticipation and trepidation. The clandestine nature of their meeting in Cancun, far from the prying eyes of law enforcement in Miami, spoke volumes about the delicate dance of power and secrecy that governed the Syndicate. It was a high-stakes game.

As Raphael Santos landed in Cancun, the anticipation of the shuttle van ride to the hotel was palpable. Silent and introspective, he was consumed with thoughts about the upcoming meeting with Gabriel. Upon arrival at the hotel, Raphael was escorted to a lavish suite where Gabriel and Michael were waiting. Gabriel's typically boisterous demeanor was noticeably subdued. When Raphael entered the room, Michael greeted him with a firm handshake, then turned to Gabriel. With a serious look, Gabriel welcomed Raphael and gestured for them to sit down, signaling the beginning of what was sure to be a significant conversation.

Gabriel started by thanking Raphael for showing up at the meeting. "Now more than ever, we need to stick together," Gabriel began, his voice low and commanding. "We may have faced setbacks, but we can't let fear paralyze us. It's time to rebuild and come back stronger."

Curiosity mingled with apprehension as the syndicate members leaned forward, eager to hear the plan. Gabriel had always been the architect of their schemes, with a vision that had made them successful thus far. Now, he hoped his ingenuity would lead them to safety once more.

"Gabriel's proposal reflects a strategic pivot in the Miami Syndicate healthcare operations, emphasizing the need for diversification in the face of the investigation and arrests made in the past months in Miami for healthcare fraud," Michael interjected. "We need to navigate very carefully and quietly. We need to diversify as we talked about in the past, to explore new avenues of profit."

Eyes widened, and hushed whispers filled the room as the members exchanged glances. Expanding beyond their well-established healthcare fraud network was risky, but they trusted Gabriel's judgment.

"We have connections, resources, and expertise that can be leveraged in other criminal enterprises," Gabriel explained. "With the right approach, we can create additional streams of income that will not only sustain us but propel us to greater heights."

Michael and Raphael nodded in agreement, while Raphael (El Chino) remained cautious. Their involvement in healthcare fraud had yielded immense wealth, but they were aware of the dangers that lurked in the streets of Miami's criminal underworld.

"We have the means to venture into illegal activities like fake credit cards, stolen fuel, and pain clinics," Gabriel continued, laying out his vision. "While some of these operations might not yield profits on par with healthcare fraud, they benefit from reduced scrutiny, allowing us to engage in street-level dealings with an elevated tolerance for risk."

As Gabriel spoke, he could see the skepticism giving way to intrigue. He knew he needed to present a compelling case to win over Michael and Raphael.

"Think about it," he urged, his voice rising with conviction. "We'll still need to be cautious, but diversifying our operations will make us more resilient. We'll withstand the blows of law enforcement and competitors alike."

Raphael raised a legitimate question, seeking clarification. "Gabriel, I understand the need to change, but isn't this more dangerous? Healthcare fraud was our specialty. Venturing into these new territories will require new contacts and alliances."

Gabriel nodded, acknowledging the valid concern. "You're right. It won't be easy, and we'll need to tread carefully. But we have built relationships over the years. Our reputation precedes us, and that will be an advantage. We'll take calculated risks, and I have plans to connect with reliable allies who can help us navigate these new waters."

The room fell silent as the crew contemplated Gabriel's proposition. The weight of their previous successes and recent setbacks hung heavy in the air. They knew that inaction would be their downfall, and Gabriel's plan presented an opportunity for survival and wealth.

"We trust you, Gabriel," Raphael spoke out. "Lead us in this new direction, and we'll follow."

With the support of his loyal followers, Gabriel felt a surge of determination. He knew the road ahead would be treacherous, but they were united by a shared vision and fierce loyalty to their leader.

"Thank you," Gabriel said, a smile tugging at the corners of his lips. "Together, we'll forge a path to prosperity, and the PMC will rise again, stronger and more formidable than ever."

As the meeting continued, Gabriel stressed the importance of loyalty and secrecy. He clarified that the PMC's survival depended on its unity and discretion.

"So, tell me," Michael spoke out with a hint of amusement in his voice, "how are we doing in the streets of Miami? Our operation seems to be like dry ice smoking, but cold." He chuckled at his analogy.

Raphael, his expression grave, replied, "The medical supply offices have been a challenging operation but like always, very lucrative. But we are making steady progress.

Our crew has successfully rented office space in several key locations."

He paused, steep-ling his fingers. "As for Miami, you're correct that the locals are wary. Too many have fallen to law enforcement they are getting hip to the game day by day they get better. We must tread carefully and build trust through our networks. I have several potential recruits in mind disgruntled professionals who can aid our money laundering efforts."

Raphael's eyes hardened. "The banks are the trickiest part. Increased security protocols make extracting large sums increasingly difficult. However, I have a plan to introduce seasonal cash businesses into the mix legal on the surface but perfect for injecting our ill-gotten gains. It will require some startup capital, but I'm confident we can make it work."

He leaned back, steep-ling his fingers once more. "Overall, the operation is progressing. Slowly, methodically. We cannot afford impatience or recklessness. Trust me to handle the details; I will ensure the Miami Syndicate operations remain firm."

"Raphael, you and I are going to be working closely on our operation in the streets of Miami," Gabriel said, leaning back in his chair. "I hope we can be truthful with each other like we spoke about in Naples."

"Of course. I value honesty and loyalty above all else. I'll be the man on the streets, Gabriel, while you pull the strings from the backroom as our mysterious mastermind. Michael, our fugitive associate, things are no better for our partner here Michael looks towards Gabriel, he has to keep a low profile for now. Raphael, again I will say this to you, please don't ever say my name I simply don't exist anywhere. Maintaining operational security is critical. Again never use my real name or any identifying details in your communications with anyone in person or especially by cellular."

Raphael Santos gave a deep stare as Gabriel Cortez outlined his new responsibilities within the Miami syndicate. He knew this second meeting multiple calls came with immense trust, but Gabriel also had given consequences if that trust was ever broken.

"Chino, find someone you can depend on with your life, someone who won't crack under pressure no matter what the cops throw at him," Gabriel instructed. "Train this person in everything you do for us. He will be the filter between you and the law."

Chino already had someone in mind. A family member who idolized him and could keep his mouth shut tighter than a clam's grip on a pearl. He would make him an offer he couldn't refuse.

"I think we covered enough in this meeting," the voice

in the room rumbled. "I'll meet you back in Miami soon. We'll go over more details then, Raphael. But for now, you have many tasks in front of you."

"Stay focused," the voice continued, a note of warning in its tone. "And stay safe."

Meanwhile, in Miami, the task force worked tirelessly, following any lead that could lead them to Michael's whereabouts. They combed through phone records, financial transactions, and surveillance footage, piecing together any fragments of information that might point them in the right direction.

"We can't let up," one detective said during a late-night brainstorming session. "We must keep the pressure on, and eventually, we'll find him."

Chapter 13

DISSOLVING DARKNESS

The court day had arrived, and the defendants took the stand one by one, pleading guilty to their participation in the corruption case. The judge set separate sentencing dates for the rogue detective, Anderson, and Raul, the restaurant owner, to give their cases the individual attention they deserved.

As Raul waited to be called, a sense of dread crept up his spine. He had spent countless nights agonizing over this moment, replaying the events that had led him here and wondering if there was anything he could have done differently.

When the time came for Raul Dominguez, the judge cleared the courtroom. Raul took a deep breath and stepped in front of the judge. The judge's gaze was stern, but Raul steeled himself, ready to take responsibility for his actions.

"Mr. Raul Dominguez, you have been charged with multiple counts of bribery, fraud, and counter-surveillance. How do you plead?"

"Guilty, Your Honor," Raul replied, his voice barely above a whisper.

The honorable Judge Robertson nodded, jotting down a few notes. "Very well. Before I determine your sentence, I will need you to provide a full testimony of your involvement in this case."

Judge Robertson, a stern-faced man with graying hair, called the courtroom to order. He turned his piercing look to the U.S. Attorney, Alice Harper, in a crisp suit.

"Mrs. Harper," he began, his voice carrying authority, "I am directing you to convene a grand jury within the next few months. The purpose is to hear testimony regarding the alleged fraudulent activities occurring in Miami's streets."

Alice Harper nodded, jotting notes furiously. "Yes, Your Honor."

"You will begin by hearing Raul Dominguez's debrief," the judge continued. "Pay close attention to what he knows, and equally important, what he doesn't know about this organization."

Mrs. Harper looked up, a question in her eyes. The judge anticipated her query.

"Yes, I said organization. We all know there's a structured group behind these fraudulent activities. Your grand jury will also hear from other witnesses who may have knowledge of or involvement in these operations."

As the judge spoke, the courtroom remained silent, the gravity of the situation palpable. The prosecutor's mind raced, considering the implications of this directive.

"The grand jury's findings will be crucial in determining our next steps," Judge Robertson concluded. "We must uncover the extent of this healthcare fraud and its impact on our city. Time is of the essence, Mrs. Harper. I expect daily updates on your progress."

The U.S. Attorney stood, her posture straight and determined. "Understood, Your Honor. I'll begin preparations immediately."

As the Honorable Judge Robertson dismissed the court, a flurry of activity erupted. U.S. Attorney Alice Harper hurried out, already making calls to assemble her team. The judge watched from his bench, his expression grim. He knew that the coming weeks would be pivotal in exposing the corruption that had taken root in Miami's streets.

As the court emptied, Julian and Jackie let out a sigh of relief. They had received the guilty pleas, and now they turned their attention to the next step: continuing the hunt for Michael Cruz.

U.S. Attorney Alice Harper had done her job, securing the convictions they had sought. Julian and Jackie were grateful for her efforts and made sure to express their heartfelt thanks as they walked out of the courtroom.

With the legal proceedings behind them, Julian and Jackie were now laser-focused on tracking down Michael Cruz. They knew he was still out there, evading capture, and they were determined to bring him to justice. The hunt was on, and they were more motivated than ever to find their elusive target.

As they stepped out into the streets of Miami, Julian and Jackie shared a knowing glance. The road ahead might be long and treacherous, but they were prepared to face whatever challenges lay in their path. They were driven by a sense of purpose, a desire for closure, and an unwavering commitment to seeing this through to the end.

The hunt for Michael intensified, the pressure mounting as detectives struggled to find any trace of the elusive fugitive. Every avenue had been exhausted, from surveilling his family to questioning associates and searching his properties. Yet, Michael seemed to have vanished into thin air, leaving only frustration and unanswered questions in his wake.

As days turned into weeks, Jackie Ortiz grew increasingly desperate. Frustration was palpable as surveillance footage was reviewed, intercepted calls listened to, and all available information on Michael's activities pieced together. The task force pinned their hopes on him making a mistake – a phone call, an email – anything to lead them to his whereabouts. Yet, their efforts yielded no results.

In a last-ditch effort, they turned to federal inmates possibly tied to the Miami syndicate. The hope was that someone within the prison walls might have a lead on Michael's whereabouts or activities. The prison harbored whispers and secrets, a microcosm of the criminal world. The detectives saw it as a potential goldmine of information, where connections and loyalties were tested in the crucible of incarceration. Their hope rested on the belief that inmates associated with the Miami syndicate might possess the missing pieces of Michael's disappearance puzzle.

Entering the prison, Detective Julian Prat and Jackie Ortiz encountered palpable tension. Survival often depended on keeping one's own counsel in this environment, where alliances shifted and trust was scarce. Navigating the corridors, they drew curious glances from inmates who recognized the law enforcement emblem.

Meeting with inmates required a delicate balance. Each interaction involved building rapport and extracting information while navigating the prison hierarchy's unspoken rules. Some inmates were wary, their words measured. Others, eager to establish connections beyond the prison walls, were more forthcoming, sharing potentially vital information about Michael's disappearance.

In a small visiting room, Detective Julian Prat sat across from an inmate whose eyes conveyed weariness and resignation. He had witnessed the rise and fall of criminal empires, the shifting allegiances, and the betrayals within these walls. His words were chosen carefully, hinting at a world of clandestine dealings and whispered conversations.

He spoke of the Miami syndicate in a quiet tone, describing its hierarchy, connections, and the unwavering loyalty binding its members. He shared stories of overheard conversations in shared cells, fragments hinting at a fugitive named Michael. Detectives listened intently, mentally piecing together information in their quest for answers.

But it wasn't solely about what was said but also about what remained unsaid. The inmates had their code, their language existing between the lines. Julian and Jackie deciphered hidden messages, nuances revealing truth amidst deception's layers. Each interaction was a puzzle, a mosaic of words and glances needing decoding to extract valuable information.

And yet, even in this world of half-truths, the detectives

sensed a genuine desire to help. Some inmates, worn down by years behind bars, were tired of the cycle of crime and punishment.

They saw an opportunity to offer a semblance of redemption, a chance to aid, and potentially receive sentence reduction.

As Julian Prat and Jackie Ortiz departed the prison, they carried a mixture of frustration and newfound hope. The inmates had provided fragments of information, pieces of a larger puzzle that was Michael's disappearance. It was now their task to meticulously piece together those fragments, decipher the hidden messages, and follow the faint trails that might lead them closer to the truth.

Weeks dragged on, and frustration turned to desperation. Just when hope seemed lost, a glimmer of potential breakthrough emerged. A call came in from a family member of a federal inmate, claiming the inmate possessed information of interest to the detectives. The task force wasted no time and arranged a visit to the Federal Correctional Center.

Sitting across from the inmate in the sterile visiting area, Detective Julian leaned forward, his gaze locked onto the inmate's eyes. "You mentioned your cellmate might have some information. Can you tell us more?"

The inmate hesitated momentarily, his eyes flickering

as if debating whether to share what he knew. Finally, he leaned in his voice barely above a whisper. "Yeah, Michael. He's part of that Miami syndicate stuff. My cellmate—he was in the Miami Correctional Center awaiting his court date, and he was with some guy who was Michael's co-defendant. They had smuggled cellular phones; he would hear them talking about him being on the run."

A chill ran down my spine. This was the break we'd been waiting for—a potential lead on the elusive Michael we'd been trying to take down for some time. "Did your cellmate mention anything else? Any details about where Michael might be hiding out?" I pressed, attempting to keep my voice level and calm.

The inmate shifted, looking around as if checking for eavesdroppers, even in this confined space. "He made it sound like Michael's gone beyond the borders, man. Said something about high-up connections getting him out of the country. And it's not just any country—they're keeping him safe, you know?"

Detective Julian leaned back, his mind racing. "So, you're saying he's not even in the U.S. anymore?"

The inmate nodded, his expression solemn. "That's what I gathered. They aren't dumb. They know the heat's on here. Michael's too valuable to let get caught."

Detective Jackie leaned forward, her tone urgent. "Did

your cellmate mention where he might be?"

The inmate shook his head, a frustrated look crossing his face. "Nah, man, they ain't stupid enough to spill specifics like that. But he did hear them say Michael's been lying low, keeping his moves off the radar."

Detective Julian exchanged another glance with his partner. "Did your cellmate say anything else? Anything that could help us locate him?" He shook his head grimly. "Nothing specific."

Detective Julian leaned forward again. "Thank you for sharing this with us. Your information could be a breakthrough."

The inmate's gaze turned intense, his voice low and serious. "Just keep my name out of this, you hear? My safety's on the line too."

Detective Julian nodded reassuringly. "You have our word.

Your cooperation won't go unnoticed."

As they left the visiting area, the detectives exchanged thoughts in hushed tones. "If Michael's truly out of the country," Detective Julian absorbed, "we've got a whole new set of challenges ahead."

But with the flicker of hope ignited by the inmate's revelations, the detectives knew they had a long road ahead.

The syndicate had proved its ability to adapt and evade, but they were determined to follow every lead, decipher every code, and ultimately bring Michael to justice – no matter where he was hiding.

Chapter 14

ENTANGLED PURSUITS

Julian and Jackie discovered that Michael Cruz had ventured far beyond South Florida's borders, delving into the depths of

Mexico's criminal underworld. His extensive network spanning different countries had kept him elusive to the law for quite some time. "It's quite apparent," Julian remarked. "There haven't been any rumors circulating on the streets of Miami. Any sightings of Michael?"

Detective Julian Pratt and his partner, Jackie Ortiz, crossed the Texas border into Mexico, pursuing a lead in their ongoing case. They had been on the trail of Michael

Cruz for a considerable period, and their determination to bring him to justice only grew stronger.

Driving through the dusty border towns, Julian couldn't shake off a sense of unease. The prevalence of cartel activity in this region was notorious, demanding extra caution. He gripped the steering wheel tightly, scanning the streets for any signs of suspicious activity.

Their first stop was a rundown motel on the outskirts of a small town. The manager, a weathered old man, eyed them warily as they flashed their badges and inquired about recent guests matching their suspect's description. After a few tense moments, the manager responded, "You're asking the wrong questions in the wrong country, especially coming from the United States. You'll get no answers from the locals."

Detective Jackie Ortiz realized they couldn't handle this alone. They reached out to their counterparts at Interpol, sharing their discoveries and seeking assistance in apprehending the fugitive. Taking their pursuit of Michael to another Level would have significant implications for their investigation.

Julian and Jackie journeyed to Mexico City for a meeting with Interpol regarding their ongoing investigation. As senior detectives, they were responsible for gathering intelligence and coordinating efforts with the international law enforcement agency.

Upon arrival at Mexico City airport, the Miami detectives proceeded directly to the Interpol office. They were greeted by Mr.

Gutierrez, the lead agent overseeing the case, who promised to provide updates as they became available.

Seated across from Mr. Gutierrez in his office, Jackie Ortiz wasted no time and began by presenting him with a comprehensive file containing all the information and photographs the Miami Task Force had gathered on their target, Michael. She explained that Michael Cruz was a fugitive they had been tracking, and they believed he was currently hiding out in Mexico.

Mr. Gutierrez responded, "Mexico is a vast country. Mexico City alone has over 20 million people. But nothing is impossible. We have many resources and a network of street-level informants. However, here in Mexico, it's a two-way street. We must proceed with extreme caution. Criminal organizations have more resources and even better counter-surveillance measures than law enforcement."

When you first contacted my office, you explained the situation that there's a fugitive hiding out in my country. I assigned a couple of agents to gather information on Michael Cruz, the person of interest.

Detectives from both sides of the border filed in, their expressions a mix of anticipation and determination. They were chosen for their unwavering commitment to justice and their proven ability to handle such operations.

As Julian and Jackie exchanged a reassuring glance as they sat at the table. The atmosphere was charged with expectancy, the weight of the mission heavy on their shoulders. The room was now filled with professionals who grasped the gravity of the task.

Guttierez stepped to the front, commanding attention. "Ladies and gentlemen," he began, his voice low and steady. "We're here to discuss a matter of utmost importance."

Heads nodded in agreement, the agents keenly aware of the significance. The officer continued, "We have credible information that Michael, the fugitive we've been pursuing, has embedded himself within a Mexican criminal organization."

A murmur of disbelief spread through the room. The implications of this revelation were vast and complex, with these organizations' influence transcending borders, and challenging law enforcement strategies.

"Our mission is twofold," the Interpol officer stated firmly. "To apprehend Michael. This is no easy task. We understand the risks."

Detective Jackie leaned forward, her voice resolute. "We've seen the havoc caused by Michael's criminal enterprises. Innocent lives have been ruined. Justice must prevail."

The officer agreed. "Indeed. But let's not underestimate our adversary's complexity. This operation demands precision, intelligence, and unwavering teamwork."

Detective Julian scanned the room, observing determined faces. "We've faced adversity before. We've taken down powerful criminals. This is no different. A common goal unites us, and we have the expertise to see it through."

The room fell into focused silence as agents absorbed their commitment's weight. The tension was palpable, a mix of determination and apprehension.

"We'll keep the operation details restricted," the Interpol officer warned, his tone grave. "Only those in this room will know our strategy. We can't underestimate Mexican criminal organizations' reach."

Outside the meeting room, life continued unaware of the storm brewing within Interpol's Mexico City office. The agents dispersed, focused on the dangerous path ahead, sharing hope their efforts would bring Michael to justice.

Interpol's involvement escalated the situation's urgency. Their combined efforts would be crucial in piercing Michael's secrecy layers. The detectives returned to Miami, working tirelessly, analyzing data, tracking transactions, and identifying safe houses.

In Miami, Sophia paced her apartment floor, her mind in turmoil. Gabriel's phone call had left her unsettled, sensing the weight of an unspoken secret he kept.

Gabriel's involvement in criminal activities set Sophia's mind racing with thoughts of their relationship. It couldn't continue like this. She loved him deeply, but the constant fear of losing him to the dangerous world he navigated weighed heavily on her heart. She had grown up in a world far removed from his, yearning for stability and normalcy.

Clutching her phone tightly, her heart pounded as Gabriel's name flashed on the screen. With a shaky breath, she answered the call.

"Hello?" Her voice trembled, anxiety and anticipation evident.

"It's me," Gabriel's voice came through, weariness and reassurance mingling in his words.

Sophia leaned back against the cushions, her eyes scanning the room for answers. "Gabriel, where are you? Are you okay?" Concern palpable.

His response measured as if choosing his words carefully. "I'm safe, Sophia. That's what matters most right now."

Relief flooded her as she closed her eyes briefly. "Thank goodness," she whispered, easing her grip on the phone.

"I know you have questions," Gabriel continued, strained but determined. "And I promise I'll explain everything. But I can't risk saying too much over the phone."

Frustration clouded Sophia's expression. "Gabriel, please, you have to tell me something. I can't just sit here in the dark."

He sighed heavily. "I wish I could believe me. But there are things I can't discuss right now."

Sophia's fingers tightened around the phone again, thoughts racing. "This isn't like you, Gabriel. To be involved in something so dangerous."

A pause, then Gabriel's voice, grappling with his response. "I know, Sophia. I know it's hard to understand. But I need you to trust me."

Tears welled up in Sophia's eyes, emotions swirling. "I do trust you, Gabriel. But I need to know you're not in over your head, or doing something that could destroy us."

His voice softened, vulnerable. "I never wanted any of this to touch you, Sophia. You mean everything to me."

Wiping away a tear, Sophia's voice trembled. "Then come back, Gabriel. Whatever it is, we'll figure it out together."

Gabriel's response was tinged with sadness. "I wish it were that simple, but I can't. Just know I'm doing everything to keep you safe."

Her heart ached, feeling the distance. "When will I see you again?" she whispered.

"I don't have an exact answer," Gabriel admitted, uncertainty echoing hers.

A heavy silence, emotions filling the void. Sophia closed her eyes, trying to steady herself.

"Promise me you'll be careful," she said, voice breaking slightly.

"I promise, Sophia. I'll do whatever it takes to make things right."

As they said goodbye, concern, fear, and a deep yearning filled Sophia. Sitting in the quiet of her apartment, she waited for the day their paths would cross again.

As the Interpol investigation intensified, they closed in on Michael Cruz's activities in Cancun. The evidence painted a disturbing picture: Michael was deeply embedded in corruption and money laundering networks, akin to the Miami Syndicate in South Florida. Yet, despite relentless pursuit, Michael remained elusive, slipping away each time authorities thought they had him cornered. He remained a smooth operator, using charm and connections to stay ahead of the law.

Chapter 15

CROSSING BORDERS OF DECEIT

As the day neared its end, the sun slowly descended toward the horizon, casting a warm and vibrant glow over the Miami skyline. Detective Julian Pratt stood in his office, deeply immersed in thought, trying to process the information just received from Interpol. The news was both promising and unsettling: their next destination in the search for Michael was Cancun, Mexico, a place fraught with danger and mystery.

Julian's forehead furrowed as he scrutinized the details, his fingers drumming anxiously on the desk. The trail had led them this far, but the prospect of venturing into such a treacherous region filled him with unease. Cartels, corruption, and violence loomed in the streets of Cancun, heightening the stakes.

Detective Jackie entered the room, her expression a blend of determination and concern. "Julian, Interpol just sent over some preliminary data. They've narrowed down a possible city and area where Michael might be hiding."

Julian looked up, meeting Jackie's gaze. "Yes, I received the same memo."

She nodded, tapping on her tablet. "Cancun. It's a tourist hot-spot, making it easy for him to blend in. The area is notorious for its underground criminal networks, a likely haven for someone like Michael."

Julian's jaw tightened as he absorbed the information. Cancun was known as a refuge for those seeking anonymity, where legality blurred with lawlessness.

"We need to proceed with caution," he said, his tone cautious yet resolute. "We can't afford to make reckless moves that could jeopardize the operation."

Jackie agreed, her gaze unwavering. "Interpol warned us about the local criminal organizations. We have to be prepared for resistance."

As they discussed their strategy, Julian couldn't shake the feeling that the stakes had reached an unprecedented level. The pressure was on to finally apprehend Michael, to close the chapter on the relentless pursuit that had consumed them for so long.

Meanwhile, Gabriel and Michael navigated through the bustling crowds of Cancun's nightlife, enveloped in its vibrant energy. Yet beneath the surface, a dangerous undercurrent lurked. Amidst the thumping beats of the club, they engaged in a hushed conversation, aware of the risks surrounding them.

Glancing over their shoulders, they maneuvered through dimly lit alleyways, wary of potential threats lurking in the shadows. The lively streets gave way to a grittier reality drug dealers prowling, occasional scuffles breaking out.

"We can't linger here," Michael's voice cut through the chaos, the neon lights illuminating their surroundings.

Gabriel nodded, acknowledging the harshness of their reality as they navigated the crowd. "This chaos is our domain, Michael. We must embrace it, leverage it to our advantage."

"With our established connections," Gabriel continued confidently, "we're poised to expand beyond healthcare fraud, exploring new avenues for power and profit."

"Our strength lies in our adaptability," Gabriel asserted, a smirk playing on his lips. "It's time to redefine our legacy, reshape it for the future."

Michael regarded him with a smile. "If our legacy is built solely on illicit crimes, then it's time for a change."

As they passed a vibrant nightclub, the music pulsed, and swaying bodies hinted at temptation. Gabriel, on a mission, found the allure too strong to resist. The energy was electric, with bodies moving in sync with the bass. With a shared hunger in their eyes, they changed direction, drawn by the promise of excitement.

Gabriel stepped into the crowded nightclub, his senses immediately overwhelmed by the intoxicating blend of perfume and alcohol hanging heavy in the air. Vibrant lights danced across the room, matching the pulsating rhythm that seemed to course through everybody on the dance floor.

Drink in hand, Gabriel surrendered to the rhythm, his body swaying with electric energy. His eyes scanned the writhing mass of dancers, searching for that spark, that magnetic pull of connection. Suddenly, time seemed to slow as his gaze locked with a raven-haired beauty, her movements hypnotic and inviting.

Drawn by an irresistible force, Gabriel approached her and her friend, his steps falling naturally in sync with theirs. The music pulsed around them, creating an intimate bubble in the chaos of the club. Their bodies moved in harmony, a wordless conversation of desire and freedom.

The air crackled with intensity as Michael, Gabriel's friend, joined their dance. The four bodies intertwined, feeding off each other's energy, creating a symphony of motion and emotion. Inhibitions melted away with each pounding beat, revealing raw, uninhibited versions of themselves.

Gabriel felt a surge of electricity as the woman's fingers grazed his arm, her touch igniting a longing he'd buried deep within. Her warm smile beckoned him closer, urging him to let go of his carefully constructed walls. Beside him, Michael laughed with unbridled joy, a side of him Gabriel had never witnessed.

As the night progressed, Gabriel realized this transcended mere physical attraction. It was a spiritual awakening, a rediscovery of the profound beauty in human connection. He saw the same epiphany reflected in Michael's eyes, in the tender way the two women supported each other.

The music slowed, but Gabriel's heart continued to race. Gratitude washed over him – for the exhilaration of the night, for the reminder that even in the most unexpected places, souls can touch and transform. As they exchanged farewell embraces, the air charged with unspoken promises and newfound understanding.

Chapter 16

CANCUN'S HUNT

The flight to Mexico was tense, filled with anticipation and uncertainty. Julian and Jackie, armed with preliminary data from Interpol, descended into the vibrant chaos of Cancun. The city's skyline emerged on the horizon, a deceptive beauty concealing lurking dangers.

Stepping out of the airport, Julian was struck by Cancun's sights and sounds. The bustling streets and undercurrent of tension contrasted sharply with the safety of Miami.

Their airport contact escorted them to an SUV, and the group set off to headquarters. Jackie dominated the conversation during the journey, while the Interpol agent remained mostly silent due to his limited English proficiency.

Julian, sitting quietly beside Jackie, struggled to formulate coherent responses. His passable Spanish allowed him to grasp the gist of her anxious monologue, but true engagement eluded him.

The ride to headquarters was tense and stilted, punctuated only by Jackie's occasional outbursts. Julian watched the cityscape flash by, his mind filled with unanswered questions and unease.

Upon arriving at the imposing government building, the Interpol agent signaled their arrival. As they entered headquarters, the weight of their shared objectives hung thick in the air.

Welcomed into the room by the stern-faced Agent Lopez, tension filled the air. They knew this encounter would be pivotal, determining the fate of their mission.

Agent Lopez assessed them, recognizing the high stakes and the necessity of success. He outlined the operation's details, emphasizing the need for absolute dedication and focus.

Julian and Jackie found themselves drawn into Lopez's intensity, united in their conviction to see the mission through. They shared a meaningful glance, their shared history strengthening their resolve.

Entering the briefing room, they listened intently as Lopez wasted no time delving into the operation's details. Their readiness was communicated through nods, they were prepared to confront whatever obstacles lay ahead.

Agent Lopez painted a vivid picture of the treacherous path ahead, but Julian and Jackie remained undeterred. They were seasoned operatives, unwilling to falter in the face of adversity.

In the room adorned with maps and surveillance photos, a clearer picture of Michael's potential whereabouts emerged. Each piece of information contributed to the puzzle, slowly forming a coherent picture.

On the largest map, there were red pins scattered along a trail, marking the neighborhoods and places Michael had supposedly visited. He had always been skilled at covering his tracks, but the network of informants and intelligence operatives had managed to trace his movements, from back alleys to clubs and restaurants.

As Agent Lopez discussed their findings, a sense of determination filled the room. Inch by inch, they were closing in on their target, growing ever closer. Michael had eluded them in the past, but this time, they felt confident that they had the upper hand. With Interpol's resources and the local police's intimate knowledge of the city's landscape, they were certain they would track him down and bring him to justice.

Although the mission was far from over, the team could feel the momentum shifting in their favor. They had come one step closer to finally putting an end to Michael's reign. The walls of the room stood witness to their collective resolve, serving as a testament to the power of collaboration and an unwavering pursuit of the truth.

Finally, the meeting came to an end. We all said our goodbyes and Julian and Jackie headed off to their respective hotel rooms.

Eager to freshen up and find a cozy restaurant for a warm meal, Julian and Jackie couldn't wait to put the long and emotionally draining day behind them. The satisfaction of a job well done filled me with energy.

As Jackie stepped into the shower, the warm water washed away the day's stresses, leaving her refreshed and rejuvenated. She was now ready to indulge in a delicious dinner. After toweling off, Jackie quickly changed into comfortable, casual clothes and made her way to the lobby to meet Julian.

Jackie Ortiz entered the elevator, and the metal doors closed softly behind her. As the floor numbers descended, she couldn't shake the feeling that something was different, a subtle change in the air.

When the elevator doors opened in the lobby, Julian stood there, waiting with his familiar, disarming smile.

"Jackie," he said, his voice filled with warmth, "you look stunning."

Feeling her stomach rumble, Julian and Jackie wandered through the bustling city streets, determined to find the perfect

Mexican restaurant for dinner. They strolled past crowded cafes on the Cancun Strip and trendy bistros, their eyes scanning each storefront for an inviting ambiance.

"There must be something good around here," Jackie said with hunger and anticipation evident in her voice.

Undeterred, Julian replied, "We'll find the right place, I'm sure of it."

As they turned the corner, a warm glow emanated from a charming establishment nestled between two buildings. The sign above the door read "Orale Guerito Grill."

"This looks promising," remarked Julian. "We did agree on Mexican."

They pushed open the heavy wooden door and immediately embraced the cozy and intimate atmosphere. Soft lighting illuminated the rich, burgundy walls and sturdy oak furnishings. In the corner, a mariachi band played a gentle melody, soothing their senses.

The hostess greeted them with a warm smile. "Table for two?"

They were led to a secluded spot near the window, offering a picturesque view of the bustling city outside. Settling into the plush, high-backed chairs, a sense of relief and contentment washed over them.

They had never spent time together outside of work, and now they found themselves alone in a romantic setting—a dimly lit restaurant in Cancun, Mexico. The soft glow of candlelight illuminated their faces as they gazed at each other, equally surprised and intrigued by this unexpected turn of events.

Jackie, usually poised and professional in the office, felt a flutter in her chest as she met Julian's warm brown eyes. He, in turn, couldn't help but notice the way the candlelight danced across her delicate features, casting an almost ethereal glow. For a moment, a comfortable silence hung between them, both unsure of how to proceed.

Suddenly, the dam burst, and the words came flowing out. They spoke passionately about their dreams, their fears, their triumphs, and their disappointments—things they had never dared to share within the confines of the workplace. Their conversation had a rawness and intimacy that left them feeling vulnerable yet strangely liberated.

As the evening progressed, the space between them grew smaller, and the air crackled with an electricity they had never experienced before. Jackie traced the outline of Julian's hand, marveling at the calloused fingers that contradicted his gentle nature. Julian, in turn, gently tucked a stray lock of Jackie's hair behind her ear, his fingertips lingering on the soft skin of her cheek.

They had always been friends and colleagues, but in this moment, they became something more—two souls connecting on a level that transcended their professional roles.

Julian interrupted the moment, knowing they couldn't let it go any further. "Jackie, I am a married woman. Though I am not happily married, I am still married. We need to go back to the way things were, keep it professional, and maintain our focus where it belongs. As much as I want this to happen, it can't."

Julian sighed, his voice filled with regret. "Let's pretend this never existed."

They exchanged a bittersweet glance, acknowledging the reality they faced. The dream had to end, and they would have to return to their respective paths, leaving their stolen moments of connection behind.

Julian's heart raced as he stared into Jackie's eyes, their bodies inches apart. The air crackled with tension, months of unspoken desire threatening to ignite. With trembling hands, Julian cupped Jackie's face, their breath mingling.

Julian's fingers traced Jackie's jawline, her touch electric. "But we've waited so long," he murmured, leaning closer.

Jackie stepped back, tears welling in her eyes. "My marriage... it's not perfect, but it's still sacred. We have to stop this."

Julian's shoulders slumped, his expression a mixture of longing and resignation. "I know. I just... I've never felt this way about anyone before."

Jackie's voice cracked. "Neither have I. But we have responsibilities, lives we've built. We can't throw it all away."

They stood in silence, the decision hanging heavy between them.

"So, what now?" Julian asked, his voice barely audible.

Jackie straightened, forcing a smile. "We go back. You to your marriage, me to my... freedom. We focus on work, on our careers."

Julian shook his head, his eyes glistening. "Pretend this never happened?"

"It's the only way," Jackie replied, her heart breaking with each word.

They shared one last, lingering look, memorizing every detail of this forbidden moment. Unspoken words passed between them. The longing, the regret, the burning passion they could never act upon. Their eyes conveyed what their hearts couldn't – a love that defied their circumstances, their commitments, and their very lives.

Chapter 17

FINDING MICHAEL

With determination etched on their faces, Miami Detectives Julian and Jackie, accompanied by Interpol officers, stepped into the bustling streets of Cancun. The vibrant city pulsed with life, but the detectives remained laser-focused on their mission: finding Michael, the elusive criminal mastermind they had been chasing for some time.

Navigating the maze of alleyways and crowded markets, the team heightened their senses, searching for any clues that could lead them to their target. The air crackled with tension as they delved deeper into Cancun's intricate underworld, encountering a web of corruption and deceit.

Aware that time was running out and they needed to return to Miami within the next couple of days, Julian and Jackie knew they faced a formidable challenge. Michael was a ghost, a master of disguise and deception, always one step ahead. However, they refused to give up, driven by an unwavering determination to bring him to justice and provide closure to the countless lives he had destroyed.

Pressing on, the detectives encountered a network of informants and shady characters, each with their agenda. They had to tread carefully, distinguishing truth from lies and constructing a mosaic of information that could lead them to Michael's whereabouts.

The streets of Cancun became their battleground, a complex labyrinth where the line between good and evil blurred. Julian and Jackie fought against time and relied on their instincts as their only weapons in this high-stakes game of cat and mouse.

The relentless pursuit weighed heavily on their shoulders, and the risk of failure loomed large. Nevertheless, with each lead they followed, the detectives inched closer to their elusive target, their resolve strengthening with every step.

As they mingled with the underworld crowd, Jackie effortlessly struck up conversations, weaving tales that intrigued and captivated her new acquaintances. Her friendly demeanor and ability to connect with people on a personal level allowed her to quickly gain their trust.

Julian Prat, on the other hand, had always been a quiet and unassuming figure. His limited grasp of the local language made him more of an observer than a talker. However, in the shadowy world of serious criminals, this very trait became his greatest strength.

As time went by, the team delved deeper into the world of criminals, gradually understanding their language and deciphering their secret signals. They uncovered the different levels of power among criminals, identifying who held the reins and who merely followed.

With every new person they encountered, Julian and Jackie learned a little more about Michael's possible whereabouts. They picked up hints and clues, slowly piecing together the puzzle of his location.

Becoming insiders, they gained the trust of those in the criminal world. This trust allowed them to gather more information, bringing them closer and closer to finding Michael. Each conversation and interaction propelled them one step closer to solving the mystery they were chasing.

One night, as Julian sat in a dark bar near his hotel, he overheard two intoxicated individuals engaged in a hushed conversation. What he heard sent chills down his spine. They spoke of someone named "Puma," a mysterious figure who operated covertly, pulling strings behind the scenes in the criminal world.

Julian's senses heightened as he listened intently. It seemed that Puma commanded respect and was not to be trifled with. Rumors suggested that this individual excelled at running criminal operations smoothly and evading detection.

Realizing the potential significance of Puma in their search for Michael, Julian resolved to investigate further. Unraveling the mystery surrounding Puma could potentially yield crucial clues about Michael's whereabouts. With determination, Julian made a mental note to dig deeper into this enigmatic figure, understanding that it could lead them closer to their target.

Curiosity piqued, Julian quietly followed the men as they left the bar, maintaining a high level of alertness. They meandered through narrow streets and deserted roads until they reached a plain building on the outskirts of town. Julian remained at a safe distance, observing them as they entered the building and heard the door close with a resounding bang.

The following day, during their routine patrol, Julian approached Interpol agent Lopez and inquired about El Puma. Lopez's response was immediate and grave.

"El Puma? Yes, I'm familiar with that name. He's a very dangerous man. If we can apprehend him, he may have information that could lead us to the elusive fugitive, Michael."

"Let's focus on finding Puma. We can start by checking the bar he frequents on the outskirts of town," Lopez suggested. Together, Lopez and Julian entered the dimly lit establishment, scanning the room until their eyes landed on a burly man sitting alone in the corner.

Approaching cautiously, the detectives displayed their badges. "El Puma, we'd like to have a word with you," Lopez stated firmly. "We have reason to believe you may possess information regarding the whereabouts of Michael, a wanted man from Miami."

The officers were scrutinized by the man, his eyes narrowing. "I haven't heard of anyone named Michael," he grumbled, taking a deliberate sip of his drink.

Leaning in, Lopez spoke in a hushed tone. "Listen, we're aware of your connections. If you help us locate this guy, I'll owe you a significant favor. You never know when you might need a favor in return."

El Puma pondered the offer, carefully considering his options. After a tense moment of silence, he finally spoke up. "Alright, I might have some information."

Based on gathered intelligence from the streets, there have been rumors circulating about a man referred to as "El Senior Cubano" who is supposedly hiding in a nearby town. The available details are scarce, but the sources appear credible.

El Cubano is an elusive figure, possibly involved in clandestine activities. The residents have been tight-lipped about his whereabouts and actions, but there are rumors suggesting sightings of him on the outskirts of the neighboring town.

The exact nature of his involvement and the reasons for his need to hide remain unclear. However, the fact that he is known solely by the alias "El Cuba-no" suggests potential Cuban ties or Cuban origin. He is deliberately maintaining a low profile for unknown reasons, but I'll contact you if I hear anything.

Meanwhile, Gabriel and Michael anxiously awaited a call from Raphael Santos. Raphael had been managing the PMC's business affairs during Michael's absence for a few months.

Gabriel had just informed Michael that he would be returning to Miami in the coming days. This news brought a sense of relief to Michael, knowing that Gabriel's return would bring much-needed leadership and stability to the Miami Syndicate.

As minutes ticked by, Gabriel's impatience grew, eagerly anticipating Raphael's call. They needed a comprehensive update on the status of ongoing operations and any pressing issues that may have arisen before Gabriel crossed the border. He wanted to avoid any surprises.

The PMC activities demanded constant oversight and prompt decision-making. With Michael on the run, Raphael Santos had been shouldering a heavy burden in maintaining smooth operations.

"Listen, Gabriel, I have something to tell you. I know you've always disagreed with my decision, but hear me out. In a few weeks, I'll be crossing over and returning to Miami, and I firmly believe it's the right choice for me," Michael expressed, his voice filled with conviction. "Gabriel, I understand your concerns—Cancun can be a dangerous place, especially for someone like me; we don't belong here, and our differences are noticeable, despite speaking Spanish. That's just one reason behind my decision. I know Miami like the back of my hand. I have connections there—family and trusted individuals who can keep me hidden."

"It might be easier for me to disappear there than it is here in Cancun," Michael continued, emphasizing his conviction. "Furthermore, I'll be able to blend in much better. Gabriel, I've thoroughly thought this through, I promise. Everything will be alright."

Gabriel's face showed concern, his brow furrowed with worry. "But I want to ensure your safety," he pleaded. "Cancun may be overwhelming, but in Miami, you'll be putting yourself in harm's way."

Placing a hand on Gabriel's arm, Michael locked eyes with him. "Sometimes, Gabriel, you just have to take a risk."

"Alright, Michael, listen carefully. You're a wanted man, a fugitive on the run, and when you cross over to Miami, you'll have to abide by a whole different set of rules. There's no room for error, do you understand?" Gabriel spoke authoritatively, providing instructions.

"First things first, you'll need burner phones, one for each person you need to communicate with. No connections between your associates can be traced. Make it as difficult as possible for anyone to track your movements or communications."

"And you'll require a dedicated driver, without exceptions. I know you believe you can handle it, but you need to exercise extreme caution—Miami is not a walk in the park. A single misstep, and it's game over. The driver must be utterly reliable; someone you trust with your life."

"Look, I understand you're accustomed to calling the shots, but this is a different ballgame. It's a serious matter. If you mess up, it won't only be your life on the line. So, follow these rules to the letter, do you comprehend? No shortcuts, no exceptions. Every aspect must be foolproof, watertight, and bulletproof."

This is not a game, Michael; it's your life. Therefore, it's crucial that you have every single detail worked out and every contingency plan in place. If you don't, it won't just be you who pays the price. Do you understand?

A few days later, Gabriel and Michael were grabbing a bite to eat from a lunch truck on the street corner when a young kid approached them.

"Hey, I've got a message for Cubita from Puma," the kid said.

Gabriel and Michael exchanged glances. "Alright, what's the message?" Michael responded.

"Some gringos have been asking questions about Michael.

They want to know where to find him," the kid replied.

Michael furrowed his brow. "So they somehow know I'm here? Damn, that's not good."

"Yeah, man. Puma said to tell you to keep a low profile and stay safe," the kid said before turning and disappearing back into the crowded street.

Gabriel took a bite of his taco, his mind racing. "Are these the feds again?"

Michael shook his head. "If these gringos are asking around, it can't be good."

The two men quickly finished their lunch, a sense of

unease settling over them.

Meanwhile, Julian and Jackie were on their flight back to Miami. As the plane touched down at the Miami airport, they stepped out into the bustling corridor. The tension between them was palpable, and the memory of their almost-moment still hung in the air.

Julian turned to Jackie, his eyes burning with passionate intensity. "I can't stop thinking about what almost happened back there. Do you feel the same way?" Jackie paused, and Julian spoke firmly, "Maybe one day we can finish what we started?"

Jackie's heart raced, torn between the desire to give in to their feelings and the weight of her vows. She looked into Julian's pleading eyes, her own emotions swirling. "We need to forget that moment," she said, her voice barely above a whisper. "I am a married woman."

The words hung in the air, a bittersweet reminder of the reality they faced. Julian felt his heart sink, disappointment washing over him. Yet, a glimmer of hope remained, for Julian knew that the spark between them was undeniable.

As they continued their walk through the airport, the two were left to grapple with the intensity of their connection, knowing that the path ahead would not be easy. However, the passionate embers ignited that day refused to be extinguished, promising a future where they might finally find the courage to explore the depths of their feelings.

Chapter 18

CLOSER THAN EVER

The Miami field office buzzed with activity as team members gathered for their daily stand-up meeting. Different investigative units mingled, engaging in hushed conversations about notorious criminals and their latest mischievous activities on the streets.

Upon the task force deputy director's arrival, silence fell over the group. With a commanding presence, the captain addressed them, "Good morning, team. Let's hear the updates. Provide me with the progress on our pending cases."

Detective Smith, the lead investigator on the high-profile jewelry heist case, stepped forward. "Sir, we've made significant headway. The surveillance footage has identified the getaway driver, and we have obtained an arrest warrant for him. Tracking down the remaining crew members has proven more challenging, but we are closing in on them."

The task force director nodded, his expression stern. "Excellent work, Sanchez. Maintain the pressure. We cannot allow these criminals to escape justice."

Detective Lorenzo, in charge of the narcotics Unit, cleared her throat. "Director, we have disrupted a major drug trafficking operation. Last night's raid resulted in the seizure of over a million dollars worth of cocaine, and we have apprehended the three individuals. The interrogation is underway, and we hope to uncover the full extent of this narcotic ring"

A murmur of approval spread through the room. The task force director Murphy's eyes narrowed, and he said, "Good, Morales. Keep me updated on any new developments. We need to ensure this individual remains behind bars for a considerable time."

During the meeting, the team members shared updates on their respective cases, each more intriguing than the last. A sense of camaraderie and determination filled the air as these experienced law enforcement professionals tirelessly worked to maintain the safety of Miami's streets.

Detective Julian Prat began to recount the details of the Miami Syndicate case, but Deputy Director Murphy of the task force swiftly interrupted him. "Stop right there. We need to discuss several matters privately. Meet me in my office after the meeting."

The task force director's tone left no room for debate, conveying his seriousness. Julian Pratt nodded in understanding, aware that whatever he was about to reveal held enough weight to warrant a private conversation.

As the meeting concluded, Julian and Jackie made their way to the deputy director's office, his mind racing with possibilities. Had he stumbled upon something that compromised protocol? Were there political implications he had not considered? The uncertainty gnawed at him, but he knew he had to face the deputy director's questions headon.

Knocking on the door, Julian and Jackie entered the office, bracing themselves for the impending discussion. Deputy director Murphy gestured for them to take a seat, the tension palpable in the air.

"Both of you, I need complete honesty regarding your knowledge of the Miami case. This is a delicate situation, and we cannot afford any missteps."

Julian Prat took a deep breath and began recounting the details, omitting nothing. He understood that the Director's response would determine the next course of action, and he and Jackie were prepared to face the consequences, whatever they may be.

"Okay, let me be clear. There are two concerning factors. I just received a call from down south, indicating that Michael Cruz is back in the States. He may be right here in Miami, so stay vigilant. Leave no stone unturned, understand?"

"However, we cannot disclose Michael's return to anyone. We've already had one team member compromise our intel before, so let's keep this information strictly confidential. The element of surprise is on our side, and we must capitalize on it. Remember, loose lips sink ships."

"I know it's tempting to share this news with everyone, but we must handle it discreetly. I'm relying on you to keep it under wraps while digging up any information without drawing excessive attention. This could be our breakthrough, but we need to be smart about it. There's no room for mistakes this time."

"Just stay alert, maintain a low profile, and uncover whatever you can. With some luck, we'll capture that elusive snake before he slips away again. I'm counting on you. Let's make this happen."

As Detectives Julian and Jackie left the Director's office, their hearts raced with a mix of disbelief and urgency. The news they had just received was like a ticking time bomb—Michael, their long-lost fugitive, was in Miami, and he was not the same person they had once known.

The task force director's words reverberated in their minds: "He is in Miami, and he has become arrogant. We must catch up with him before he eludes us once more." The weight of the responsibility hung heavily in the air, compelling Julian and Jackie to act swiftly.

Meanwhile, on the opposite side of the city, Gabriel Ramirez and Raphael Santos occupied a park bench at Tropic Park in South Miami. Their hushed tones concealed the illicit nature of their conversation. Raphael Santos wasted no time and got straight to the point. "We now have three offices up and running, fully staffed with our recruits. They are generating a steady stream of patients, yielding substantial profits from insurance companies."

Gabriel nodded, his eyes narrowing with determination. "And what about the recruits? How is the recruitment process progressing?"

Raphael Santos replied a hint of pride in his voice, "It's expanding rapidly. We currently have eight individuals on standby, all willing to bend the rules to fill our pockets."

The two men chuckled darkly, fully aware that their fraudulent healthcare scheme was flourishing, sacrificing medical ethics for the allure of illicit gains. "Perfect," Gabriel said, clasping his hands together. "Continue recruiting and ensure the offices keep churning out the bills. We will milk this cash cow for all it's worth."

Raphael grinned in agreement. "Consider it done. This will be a significant score." listen Gabriel while you were approaching, I noticed a fidgety demeanor and furrowed brow. Concerned, Raphael asked Gabriel, "You seem troubled, Gabriel. It's evident on your face. What's wrong?"

Gabriel sighed, his expression grim. "Everything is going according to plan, but I have some reservations about Michael. He's on his way here."

Raphael's eyes widened in alarm. "Wasn't he supposed to stay at the safe house in Naples? I specifically advised him to remain there, but now he wants to come to Miami."

Gabriel's frustration was evident in his voice. "That could introduce numerous problems and attract unwanted attention to our operation."

"Damn it, Michael never listens," Raphael muttered, pinching the bridge of his nose. "Does he realize the risks he's subjecting us all to? We've been running a tight ship here, and a single misstep could bring everything crashing down."

Gabriel shook his head, expressing his exasperation. "No, he doesn't. You know how impulsive he is, always thinking he's invincible. I told him to stand down, but you know how that usually goes."

Raphael emitted a bitter laugh. "It's like talking to a brick wall. We must find a way to stop him before he exposes our entire operation. We cannot afford any mistakes, especially considering all the effort we've invested."

Gabriel hopped into his red Porsche and accelerated down the deserted highway. His next destination was to see Sophia, but he couldn't bring himself to reach out to her since his return. Business took precedence; distractions were out of the question.

Guilt gnawed at him. Sophia had been his closest confidante, the one person who understood him better than anyone else. However, after what he had done, how could he face her? The weight of shame burdened Gabriel's shoulders, a solitary load to bear.

With each passing mile, Gabriel's mind raced. Would Sophia even want to see him? Had she moved on, forging ahead with her life without him? Uncertainty filled him with dread. He had hurt her before, and the thought of repeating that pain was almost unbearable.

Yet, he knew he had to see her, even if it was too late, to try and make amends. Sophia deserved an explanation and a chance to understand why he had disappeared for so long. At the very least, Gabriel owed her that much.

Pulling into The Valet parking at the building where

Sophia worked in Brick-ell, near downtown Miami, Gabriel took a breath, preparing himself for the confrontation. He knew he had to face it head-on, no more running, no more hiding. It was time to confront his past and hope that Sophia would be willing to forgive him.

As he waited in the lobby, he tightly gripped the dozen roses he had brought. Each minute felt like an eternity as the clock ticked by. He anticipated that she would come out for her usual lunchtime break any moment now.

This was the moment he had dreaded and anticipated simultaneously. Would she accept his gesture, or would she reject him outright, crushing any hope he had of reconciling their tumultuous relationship?

The elevator chimed, and there she was his beloved, striding purposefully towards the exit. This was his chance. He gathered his nerves and stepped forward, extending the roses.

"Sophia, I need to talk to you," he uttered, his voice filled with remorse. "I've made a mistake, and I'm so sorry. I brought these for you as a peace offering."

Sophia stopped in her tracks, her eyes widening at the sight of the flowers. For a brief moment, he dared to hope. However, her expression hardened her jaw setting.

"I don't have time for this, Gabriel," she said icily. "Whatever you have to say, save it. I'm done."

With those words, she turned and walked away, leaving him standing there with a shattered heart and the roses hanging limply in his hand. He had staked everything on this last-ditch effort, and he had lost. The battle was over before it even began.

As Sophia walked towards the employee's parking garage, Gabriel turned around and headed towards the front of the building. The valet attendant stood by the entrance, ready to assist the next arriving guest.

Passing through the lobby, Gabriel noticed a row of chairs lining the walls. Without hesitation, he placed the bouquet of roses in one of the vacant seats, a silent gesture that felt right at that moment.

Continuing his path towards the exit, Gabriel couldn't help but feel a twinge of introspection. The flowers once intended for Sophia, now sat alone in the lobby, symbolizing their unresolved connection and missed opportunities.

Driving down Brick-ell Avenue, Gabriel admired the breathtaking view of the Miami skyline when his phone suddenly rang. Glancing down, he saw an unfamiliar number displayed on the screen. Instinctively, he chose not to answer, letting the call go to voicemail.

Something about the unknown caller made him uneasy. In a time of constant connectivity, unsolicited calls from strange numbers often hinted at potential scams, phishing attempts, or other malicious activities. Gabriel couldn't shake the feeling that engaging with this unknown party would only lead to trouble.

That evening, as Gabriel scrolled through his missed calls, his thumb hovered over the unfamiliar number, tempted to delete the voicemails without a second thought. However, something compelled him to listen a gut instinct, perhaps, or simply morbid curiosity. To his utter shock, it was Sophia's voice on the other end.

Passion coursed through Gabriel's veins as he listened to the message in his voicemail, his heart pounding.

In her message, Sophia explained in detail how she had walked to her car, her mind racing, unable to shake the feeling that she needed to go back. Something deep inside compelled her. Sophia hurriedly returned to the lobby, hope flaring in her chest.

Pushing through the doors, Sophia's eyes desperately scanned the area. But all that greeted her was a sight that made her breath catch a dozen roses, their vibrant petals silently declaring their presence, resting on a lone chair.

As Gabriel listened to Sophia's voice message for the second time, her words resonated with vulnerability and longing. As the message came to an end, he saw the number appear on the screen. Without hesitation, Gabriel answered, "Hello, Sophia."

Sophia's voice trembled as she replied, "I don't know what to do, but I can't help myself. I want to see you." Gabriel's heart ached at the pain in Sophia's words. With gentle understanding, he responded, "I want to see you as well. We need to figure this out together."

The compassion in Gabriel's tone served as a soothing balm, offering Sophia a sense of comfort and safety. Gabriel knew that whatever challenges they faced, they would navigate them with empathy and care for one another.

"I'm here, Sophia," Gabriel said reassuringly, "and I'm not going anywhere. We'll find a way to make this work, I promise."

Gabriel and Sophia allowed the silence to speak, their unspoken connection palpable in the air. At that moment, they both knew that their bond was stronger than any obstacle that stood in their way.

Chapter 19

MIAMI SYNDICATE UNVEIL

Gabriel, working out at the gym in his apartment building, received a call on his cloned cellular phone, a number known only to Michael. "What's up, Mike? Let's meet up. We need to discuss a few important matters that require attention," Gabriel replied. "Sure, let's meet for happy hour at Coconut Grove Bar and Marina," Michael suggested.

As Michael entered the bustling bar and marina, the familiar sounds of clinking glasses and lively conversations immediately filled the room. His eyes scanned the area until they landed on Gabriel, seated in his usual corner spot with his back against the wall, attentively observing the entrance. Michael couldn't help but chuckle, knowing that some things never changed. Gabriel, his old friend, and a seasoned wise guy, always maintained a protective stance, sizing up everyone who walked through the door. It was a habit deeply ingrained from his years navigating the gritty underworld.

Michael eagerly desired to become more involved in the activities of the Product Manipulation Crew (PMC), just as he had been before becoming a fugitive. He took a seat at the bar and ordered a strong drink, eager to catch up with Gabriel. As the amber liquid burned his throat, memories of their wild days in Cancun flooded their conversation— the adventurous escapades, the wild parties that lasted all night, and the exhilarating rush of adrenaline. Lost in the hazy nostalgia, they both chuckled, relishing those days gone by.

However, their conversation soon shifted to business. Michael confessed his desire to be part of the action once again, to experience the thrill and excitement in his life. Gabriel understood and quickly reassured him, "I get it, man. I give you your share every month from our dealings. But realistically, you're still a fugitive. They're looking for you at every corner."

Gabriel's expression turned serious as he continued, "We can't afford investigators stumbling upon our operation. We need to exercise extreme caution, both for our sakes if we want to maintain the prosperity of PMC." The weight of their situation began to sink in as they ordered another round, and the two friends fell into a solemn silence, each lost in their thoughts about the high-stakes game they were playing.

"I want to ask you something, and I expect an honest answer. Did you have a relationship with Nancy, Randy's wife?" Gabriel inquired. Michael remained silent for a few minutes before responding, "Yes."

Gabriel glanced at him from the corner of his eye and questioned, "I don't understand. Why would you involve yourself with a married woman? Wasn't Randy also involved in our illegal business dealings?"

"That's a cardinal sin," Gabriel continued. "The precautions we have in place make it nearly impossible for us to be implicated in any crime. Yet, you risked it all for the lust of a woman?"

Michael shifted uncomfortably, his wings folding tightly against his back. "She wasn't just any woman, Gabriel. Nancy was...different. I couldn't resist her charms."

Gabriel shook his head, his expression grave. "You know the rules. We are held to a higher standard. Our kind cannot afford such indiscretions, no matter how tempting the prize."

Michael remained silent, the weight of his actions

sinking in. He understood the risks he had taken, but the allure of Nancy had been overwhelming. Now, as the consequences threatened to unravel their carefully constructed web, he realized the gravity of his mistake.

The two friends sat in tense silence, each wrestling with the implications of Michael's indiscretion. The high-stakes game they had been playing now seemed more precarious than ever, and they both knew that the fallout could be catastrophic.

Gabriel glanced over at Michael with a pensive expression. With a sly smile, he laid his cards on the table and let out a chuckle. "Michael, you crazy bastard. I hope Nancy was worth it," he said, shaking his head. "When I heard about you and Nancy, I nearly spit out my drink. I should have suspected something when you suddenly had to take that 'extended business trip.' Were you running from the law or perhaps from your wife?"

"Listen, Michael, at the end of the day, you're my brother in crime, and we're in this PMC thing for life, you know?" Gabriel continued. "Without you, none of this would have happened. We built this organization from the ground up together."

He leaned back in his chair, a mix of pride and contemplation on his face. "This organization is going to outlast us, man. We've established a solid structure and a well though-tout plan. It's our legacy, you and me. And it will endure long after we're gone."

Gabriel reached out and gave Michael's shoulder a firm squeeze. "No matter what happens, this will always be ours. We did this, bro. And I wouldn't have it any other way." Gabriel glanced at his watch. "I have to head out soon. I'm meeting up with Sophia for dinner. Be careful, Michael. Always watch your back."

Gabriel and Sophia stepped into the dimly lit restaurant, tension palpable between them. They slid into a booth, avoiding eye contact as Gabriel focused on the menu, their fingers nervously tapping against the laminated surface. Unspoken words hung heavily in the air, the weight of Gabriel's confession burdening them both.

After what felt like an eternity, Gabriel broke the silence. "Alright, Sophia, I needed some time alone. That's all it was. I wasn't with anyone... I was alone. It's not what it seems."

Sophia finally met Gabriel's gaze, searching for any signs of deception. The vulnerability in Gabriel's voice tugged at Sophia's heart. She desperately wanted to trust her partner, to believe that everything was as straightforward as Gabriel claimed.

"And what is it, Gabriel?" Sophia's tone carried a mix of concern and accusation. "Because from where I'm sitting, it certainly appears that you've been keeping something from me."

Gabriel's gaze faltered, absentmindedly toying with the edge of the menu. "I... I've been going through a lot lately, you know? I needed some space to figure things out on my own. I never meant to make you worry."

Gabriel let out a heavy sigh, feeling the fight drain from his body. He reached across the table, cautiously placing his hand over Sophia's. "You know you can talk to me, right? Whatever it is, we'll face it together."

Sophia released a deep sigh, the fight leaving her body. "Gabriel, let me explain something to you. When you showed up at my office that day, I couldn't believe my eyes. At first, excitement overwhelmed me, but then a wave of horror washed over me, knowing that it was you. So, I walked away. Yet, I couldn't shake my thoughts. I returned because I wanted to know who you truly are."

She paused, gathering her thoughts. "You were the man I loved, the one I thought I knew better than anyone else. But the news about your friend Michael's fraud scheme shattered everything. I have so many questions in my mind. Who is the man I loved? Was any part of our relationship real, or was it all a lie? And what about your friend Michael did you conspire with him?"

Sophia's eyes searched Gabriel's face, desperate for answers. "I need to understand, Gabriel. I need to know the truth, no matter how painful it might be. Because the man I thought I knew wouldn't be capable of such deceit and betrayal. So, please, help me make sense of this. Who are you?"

The weight of her words hung heavy in the air, a palpable tension filling the space between them. Gabriel's expression was unreadable, a mix of emotions flickering across his features. It was a moment of reckoning, a chance for him to lay bare his soul and confront his past.

"Look, I'm just going to lay it out straight for you. Michael is my longtime friend, and our relationship has always been one of mutual support and understanding. While I am aware that he has been involved in some questionable activities, I have made a conscious decision to separate his personal choices from our friendship.

"My role as a friend is not to judge or go into the details of his actions, but rather to offer a listening ear and a shoulder to lean on when needed. I do not condone any illegal or unethical behavior, but I also believe that true friendship transcends the flaws and mistakes of an individual.

"Regardless of what Michael may or may not have done, I will continue to be there for him as a supportive presence in his life. This does not mean that I will aid or abet any unlawful activities, but rather that I will provide emotional support and encouragement for him to make positive changes, should he choose to do so.

"It is important to understand that my loyalty lies in our friendship, not in any specific actions or choices he has made. While I may not have direct knowledge of the details of his alleged fraudulent activities, I will not betray the trust he has placed in me by exposing personal information or speculating on matters that are not my concern.

"Sophia, my sweetheart, you need to trust me if we're going to make this work. That's why I'm here, looking deep into your eyes once more. My passion burns for you as I reach out, caressing your soft cheek, feeling that familiar spark between us. 'Look at me,' I whisper, your beautiful eyes locking with mine. 'I'm an open book before you. You can see into my soul. There are no more secrets, no more lies between us.'"

Sophia should have known better, but her heart betrayed her once again as she found herself looking into Gabriel's eyes. The passion and desire she felt were undeniable, despite all her attempts to move on.

"I miss going out to clubs and dancing with you," she admitted, squeezing his hands. "And then going back to your apartment..."

Gabriel smirked, already knowing where this was heading. "Where I would give you one of my legendary massages?"

Sophia bit her lip. Those nights of letting loose on the dance floor, dripping with sweat and relaxed, only to have his strong hands work out every kink and knot afterward—it was the pure pleasure Sophia hadn't experienced since their breakup.

Part of Sophia knew she was being reckless and irrational. Gabriel was her ex for a reason. But the chemistry between them was as explosive as ever.

"Just one more night?" she gave him a mischievous grin. "For old time's sake?"

Gabriel didn't need to be asked twice. He pulled Sophia close until she could feel his breath on her skin. "You know I can never resist you, baby girl."

Their lips collided with fervent hunger. Sophia cursed her weak heart, but there was no stopping this relapse into hot passion.

Gabriel looked at Sophia with intense eyes. In a low tone, he asked, "Are you saying this is our last night together?"

Sophia smiled. "If this is our last night, I want to do it right. I want to relive our first night together." She stepped closer, running her fingers along his chest. "Let's go dancing again like we did when we first met. Take your time and build up our desire for one another. Let's make it a night we'll never forget."

Without a word, Gabriel took her hand and led her outside to his red Porsche. They sped off towards the fluorescent lights and pulsing Latin rhythms of their favorite salsa club across from the Miami airport.

From the moment they stepped inside the club, sparks reignited between Gabriel and Sophia. The pulsating salsa beats seemed to course through their veins, drawing them to the dance floor.

Gabriel pulled Sophia close, their bodies molding together as if made for this moment. Her curves pressed against his toned frame, igniting a blazing desire that had been simmering beneath the surface for far too long. His hand traced the small of her back, guiding her through sensual movements as they moved seamlessly across the floor.

Their eyes locked, smoldering with longing and unspoken promises. Sophia's gaze dared him to go further, challenging him to push all boundaries. Gabriel's lips curved into a devilish smirk, accepting the invitation as he dipped her low, his breath hot against the sensitive skin of her neck.

In that heated embrace, the pounding beats, shouts of encouragement from fellow dancers, even the sticky humidity in the air – it all became white noise. All that mattered was the connection between them, the undeniable pull that had them chasing the highs and lows of their passionate dance.

With every dip, twirl, and roll of her hips against his, tension built to a boiling point. Sophia's fingers trailed along his neck, sending shivers down his spine. Gabriel's grip on her waist tightened possessively, silently staking his claim.

By the time the final, thunderous beats faded, they were both panting, chests heaving with the effort of restraining the raging desire that threatened to consume them whole. The magnetism between them was undeniable, the promise of the night yet to unfold hung heavy in the charged air.

Sophia's eyes smoldered with unrestrained lust as she looked up at Gabriel. His broad chest rose and fell with each ragged breath, muscles rippling beneath his shirt. The music still throbbed through their veins, fueling the primal hunger chipping away at their self-control.

"Lead the way, Gabriel," Sophia purred, biting her lip. Grabbing his hand, she followed him out of the crowded club into the cool night air. Sexual tension crackled between them like a live-wire.

As soon as they stumbled through his apartment door, Sophia pinned him against the wall, her body flush against his. Desire coursed through her veins as their lips crashed together in a fevered kiss. Hands roamed hungrily over trembling forms, tearing at clothing until it lay strewn across the bed.

Gasping for air, they clung to each other, a sweaty tangle of limbs on the bed. Raw need overwhelmed any lingering inhibitions as they moved together with increasing urgency. The bed creaked in rhythm with their passionate thrusts until they finally shattered, crying out in unforgettable ecstasy.

Sophia collapsed atop Gabriel's heaving chest with a satisfied sigh. She traced lazy circles across his slick skin as he combed his fingers through her tousled hair. Though deliciously spent, smoldering embers still glowed in their eyes.

Gabriel lay motionless on the bed, sheets tangled around his legs, as Sophia stepped out from under the covers. With casual indifference, she gathered her clothes and headed for the bathroom, the sound of running water filling the silence.

When she emerged, towel wrapped around her body, Gabriel watched her every move with a mixture of curiosity and apprehension. Sophia took her time getting dressed, purposefully avoiding his gaze.

Finally, she settled on the edge of the bed. "What are you doing?" Gabriel asked, his voice thick with unease.

Sophia turned to face him, her eyes resolute. "I'm not going to spend the night, Gabriel. I'm going to do what

I came here to do. I'm going to finish this my way." She paused, letting the weight of her words sink in. "This is my ending, not yours. And I'm also going to tell you what I came here to say."

Gabriel felt his heart pounding in his chest. He had always known this day would come, but nothing could have prepared him for the finality in Sophia's tone.

She took a deep breath. "We've been dancing around this for too long. I can't keep pretending that what we have is enough for me anymore." Her gaze locked with his, unflinching. "I want more, Gabriel. I want a real commitment, a future together. And if you can't give me that, then I have to walk away."

The room fell silent, save for the muffled sounds of traffic outside. Gabriel searched Sophia's face, looking for any hint of hesitation, any shred of doubt. But there was none.

"I love you," he said finally, the words feeling hollow and inadequate. "But I don't know if I can give you what you want."

Sophia nodded slowly, her expression a mixture of sadness and resignation. "Then I guess this is goodbye." She rose from the bed, gathering the last of her belongings.

Gabriel watched helplessly as she moved towards the door, every fiber of his being screaming at him to stop her, to say something – anything – to make her stay. But the words wouldn't come.

And just like that, she was gone, leaving Gabriel alone with the echoes of their shattered relationship and the realization that some endings are inevitable, no matter how much we may wish them away.

Chapter 20

TOO MANY SECRETS

Jackie Ortiz tightly gripped the steering wheel as she pulled out of her driveway, with the rising sun peeking through the trees. It was another day, another fruitless attempt to bring Michael to justice. Navigating the familiar route to her office in downtown Miami, her mind couldn't stop dwelling on the frustration of Michael's case. How could he still be out there after all this time? The thought gnawed at her, fueling a growing sense of determination mixed with anger.

She had dedicated her time to tracking Michael down, following every lead, and interviewing countless witnesses.

Yet, Michael always seemed to be one step ahead, vanishing into thin air before she could get close. It was maddening. Jackie knew she should let it go and focus on the other cases that demanded her attention.

Pulling into the parking lot, Jackie took a deep, steadying breath. It was time to start another day's work. But today, her focus would be laser-sharp. Michael's luck was about to run out. Jackie had one last resort, one last bullet in the gun – one she never wanted to use. However, circumstances had left her no choice. She had to reveal the secrets she had kept hidden for so long. She knocked on Julian's office door, walked in, and went over the plan with him.

"Julian, listen. I've always been against the idea of speaking to Michael's wife, but I'm out of options. My frustration and burning desire to catch him have reached a breaking point," Jackie explained. Julian replied, "I have always been open to approaching Michael's wife and telling her what she doesn't know. Maybe we can get her to open up about her husband."

Detective Ortiz sat in her car, carefully observing the suspect's house. She knew this was a delicate situation that required patience and precision. Finally, the moment she had been waiting for arrived as the suspect exited the house alone.

Approaching Michael's wife in the driveway as she was

getting into her car, Detective Ortiz spoke up. "Hello, do you remember me?" she asked. The wife responded that she did not recall.

"I'm Detective Ortiz, one of the officers who came to your house looking for Michael your husband," the detective explained, showing her badge. "Would it be okay if I asked you a few questions?"

Nancy Cruz 26yearold 5'5" Latina busty with brown wavy hair hesitated. "I don't want to talk to anyone," she said. Then she added, "Did you find something interesting that I should know about?"

Detective Jackie Ortiz paused, considering her next move. "We may have some findings that could be relevant. Would you be willing to come down to the station and discuss them with me?"

Nancy looked uneasy. "I'm not sure. Do I have to?"

"No, it's completely voluntary," Jackie assured her. "But I think it would be worth your time. There are a few things I'd like to go over with you."

Nancy thought it over for a moment. "Alright, fine. Lead the way," she said, closing her car door and following the detective.

Detective Jackie Ortiz welcomed Nancy Cruz into his office and offered her a cup of water or coffee, which she politely declined. "No thank you," Nancy responded, her voice tinged with concern. "What is it that we're here to talk about?"

Jackie replied, her tone grave and the weight of the situation palpable in the room. "Nancy, I'm afraid we need your cooperation to help us find Michael."

Jackie slid a manila envelope across the desk, signaling the seriousness of the matter.

Jackie's voice took on a serious tone as she slid the manila envelope across the desk. "These photos were taken outside the Rit hotel," she said, her voice filled with gravity. "I think you'll find them quite enlightening."

With a growing sense of trepidation, Nancy Cruz slowly opened the envelope and spread the photos out before her. Clear as day, the images revealed her husband Michael entering the hotel with another woman. They appeared comfortable and intimate, strolling through the lobby together.

Nancy's heart raced as she examined each photo, her mind spinning with a whirlwind of emotions betrayal, heartbreak, anger. After years of marriage, the seemingly solid foundation of her relationship now felt shaken to the core.

She replayed memories in her mind, searching for any signs, any clues that might have foreshadowed this infidelity.

But Michael had always been attentive, affectionate or so she thought. Now it all felt like an elaborate facade, a cruel deception.

Tears welled up in Nancy's eyes as she grappled with the harsh reality before her. How could the man she trusted most, the one she had built a life with, betray her in such a devastating way? The knowledge that he had been unfaithful cut deep, leaving her feeling foolish, insecure, and utterly heartbroken.

A mixture of disappointment and disbelief twisted Nancy's stomach. This revelation contradicted everything Michael had told her about the strength and stability of their marriage. Had Michael been deceiving her all along?

Examining the photos more closely, Nancy noticed details that seemed to corroborate the detective's findings. The body language between Michael and the other woman was relaxed and familiar, suggesting a well-established relationship beyond a chance encounter.

Taking a deep breath, Nancy spoke in a hushed tone, aware of the potential danger. "If I tell you this, it must stay between us. My life could be in danger, but not because of anything Michael would do. I'm scared of his associates or anyone else who might be involved."

Pausing, Nancy Cruz looked around nervously before continuing. "You have two options," she said, her voice low and serious.

"Michael visits his grandmother's grave every two weeks to leave theater tickets for himself and the kids," Nancy revealed. "Despite being on the run, he maintains this ritual as a way to stay connected to his family."

During each visit, Michael arrived at the cemetery at dusk, cautiously approaching his grandmother's plot. Placing the tickets in a flower vase, he hoped this small gesture would grant him a brief moment with his children during the performance.

"He usually disguises himself with glasses, a hat, and a fake beard," Nancy added. "Please, don't do anything in front of my kids, Jackie. I promise, and thank you."

Leaving the office, Nancy felt the weight of the day lifting from her shoulders. As she made her way to the elevator, Jackie approached Julian with an assertive glint in her eyes.

"Julian," Jackie declared confidently, "we've got him now. It's over."

"Let's dispatch the surveillance team to the cemetery immediately," Jackie instructed.

As the surveillance field agent, Jackson, anxiously reported the lack of progress in the Michael case to his partner Jackie Ortiz, she remained steadfast in her conviction.

"I'm sure we're on the right track, Jackson. No suspicious characters and the only person who has been near that area is the maintenance guy tending to the old flowers," Jackie reassured him.

"But it's been a whole week, Jackie. Are you certain we haven't been played?" Jackson pressed, his worry evident.

"Positive. Let me take a look at the report from Team B." Jackie reviewed the details. "Wait a minute, the report says the maintenance guy was the only one who approached the headstone in that area. But something doesn't seem right."

Sensing her partner's unease, Jackie suggested, "I think we need to take a closer look at the surveillance footage. Let's head over to the van and see what we can find."

Once at the surveillance van, Jackson, the tech specialist, greeted them. "Hey, guys. I've been reviewing the footage, and you're not going to believe this. The maintenance guy didn't just remove the flowers he also placed something in one of the vases!"

Jackie Ortiz and Julian Pratt exchanged a knowing glance. "Let's take a closer look," Jackie said.

The detectives hurried over to examine the evidence. Sure enough, discreetly tucked among the fresh flowers, they found a small Ziploc bag. "B team must have missed this. How on earth did they overlook that?" Julian exclaimed.

Jackie let out a sigh of relief. "It's fine, we've got it now. Take some pictures of those tickets and put them back. Looks like we're going to the movies next Sunday at 3:00 pm."

Chapter 21

AT THE MOVIES

On a Sunday afternoon in Miami, Task-Force (TUFF) initiated their operation to capture the notorious criminal, Michael Cruz. Months of tracking had led them to this moment, and they were determined to bring him down once and for all.

Near the theater in Coconut Grove, the team gathered, strategically parking their vehicles about a mile away in preparation for the operation. Anticipation filled the air as the agents huddled together, finalizing their plan of attack.

The surveillance team stationed outside Michael's

house carefully monitored the situation. Suddenly, the garage door opened, and her minivan drove out with her teenage kids inside. Unaware of the detectives tailing her, Nancy headed toward the movie theater.

The backup team immediately noticed the second vehicle leaving Nancy's garage. They quickly called Jackie to inform her that they were now in pursuit of this additional vehicle. Jackie acknowledged the update and instructed the team to maintain discreet surveillance on both vehicles. She wanted to ensure they had a complete understanding of Nancy's movements and any potential connections to the ongoing investigation.

The detectives followed Nancy's minivan at a safe distance, carefully monitoring her driving behavior and any stops or interactions along the way. Meanwhile, the backup team shadowed the second vehicle, ready to provide support if necessary.

As Nancy dropped off her kids at the theater, the detectives closely monitored her movements. Instead of returning home, she drove towards Key Biscayne, intriguing the detectives who discreetly followed her, eager to uncover her destination.

Upon reaching the scenic key, Nancy parked her car, overlooking the tranquil Biscayne Bay and the Miami skyline. The detectives parked nearby, ensuring they maintained visual contact without attracting attention.

Nancy appeared calm and composed as she settled in, gazing out at the serene waterfront. The detectives watched intently, pondering the reason behind her impromptu trip. Was she meeting someone? Engaging in clandestine activities? Or merely seeking a moment of solace away from her family?

Inside the theater, the atmosphere was charged with excitement as the teens entered. The crowd buzzed with anticipation for the latest blockbuster film. Unbeknownst to them, the seemingly helpful theater employees guiding them to their seats and selling snacks were undercover agents.

As the lights dimmed and the opening credits rolled, tension filled the air. The audience, a mix of eager moviegoers and skeptical critics, settled into their seats.

Meanwhile, Michael grew impatient inside the crowded theater, fidgeting in his seat. He tore open a bag of buttery popcorn and hastily stuffed a handful into his mouth.

Ten minutes into the movie, the detectives seated in Theater 6 discreetly called in to report, "Michael is not here. Our target is a no-show."

Jackie's hand trembled as she tightly gripped her cellular phone. "Team B, this is Jackie. I need you to approach Nancy's car immediately. I must speak with her."

The detectives in the unmarked car exchanged

concerned glances. "Copy that, Jackie. We're on it." They drove up and pulled alongside Nancy's vehicle.

To their astonishment, they discovered that it wasn't Nancy behind the wheel, but her younger sister, who bore a striking resemblance to her. Panic surged through their chests.

"This isn't Nancy," the detectives breathlessly informed Jackie. "We've been double-crossed."

The tension grew as the opening credits rolled, and Mich squirmed in his seat, sensing something was amiss. His gaze darted around, searching for any signs of trouble. Suddenly, a voice whispered in his ear, "Don't even think about it, Michael." He spun around to find Nancy, his wife, disguised as an innocent moviegoer.

Michael speaks firmly and in a low tone voice Nancy "Where are the kids, have you gone crazy? You're going to lead the feds to me and get me caught!" he cried. Nancy replies, "The feds approached me and showed me evidence of you cheating, you bastard. Out of anger, I told them how to find you, how you communicate with the kids."

Nancy paused, the weight of her actions sinking in. "But I couldn't go through with it, Michael. You're the father of my children, and hurting you would only amplify their pain if you get caught and go to prison."

The harsh reality hit Nancy like a ton of bricks. In a

moment of desperation, she had contemplated unthinkable actions—harming the man she had once loved, the man who had given her two beautiful children whom she cherished above all else.

Nancy's expression softened, vulnerability creeping in. "And for what it's worth, Michael, I still have feelings for you. I will always love you, no matter what happens. Not as your wife, because you betrayed me, but as the mother of our children. And I'm here to warn you—get out of Miami. They're coming down hard, and they're determined to find you."

Nancy's words caught him off guard. After all these years, the raw emotion behind them was palpable. Michael averted his gaze, weighed down by the burden of his past mistakes. "I never meant to hurt you, Nancy. You have to believe that," he said, his voice low and thick with regret.

Nancy shook her head, tears welling in her eyes. "I let my jealousy get the best of me instead of just talking to you. I'm so sorry." As she walked away, crying, her only words were a plea for him to be careful.

Meanwhile, Jackie contacted their backup team C, who had been tailing a second car leaving Nancy's garage shortly after Nancy had supposedly departed. The team responded, "At the moment, we're parked outside a mall near downtown Miami. There's only one way in and one way out of the parking garage—we've got it covered. We didn't follow the suspect inside the garage, so we didn't see who was driving."

Julian Pratt interjected, "Guys, I have a question—does that mall have a theater?"

The detectives confirmed, "Yes, there is a theater in that mall."

Jackie took a deep breath, connecting the dots. "Okay, we've got a second car leaving Nancy's house shortly after she did. And there's a theater inside the mall."

Julian exclaimed with excitement, "That's it! We need to dispatch all units to that location. That's where Michael is!"

Adrenaline surged through Jackie as she felt a thrill of excitement. "Yes, sir! This is it—we're finally going to apprehend that elusive criminal once and for all." Jackie turned to Julian, a triumphant grin stretching across her face.

As Julian and Jackie pulled into the parking lot, they could see backup units surrounding the mall, with some agents making their way toward the theater entrance. "Alright, let's do this," Jackie said, her voice laced with determination.

Julian and Jackie swiftly exited their vehicle, weapons drawn, and joined the growing contingent of agents and

Miami-Dade police as they made their way into the crowded shopping center. Jackie's heart raced with anticipation. After months of pursuing Michael, they were finally on the verge of apprehending him.

Upon reaching the main doors of the theater, they fanned out, spreading across the area to sweep it. Jackie's eyes scanned the panicked shoppers and moviegoers, searching for any sign of their target. The chaotic atmosphere, filled with screams and commotion, intensified the tension in the air.

Finally, Michael emerged from the crowd just as everyone was attempting to exit the theater. He was right there, right in front of them.

"There he is!" Julian yelled, and the chase began. Jackie sprinted after the suspect, her lungs burning and every muscle straining. This was the climax of their long pursuit.

As they closed in, Michael desperately tried to break free, elbowing and shoving his way through terrified bystanders. However, Jackie and Julian remained relentless, driven by an unwavering sense of justice.

Michael could feel the adrenaline coursing through his veins as he darted between onlookers, his heart pounding in his ears. He knew he had to escape. The police were closing in, and this was his last chance.

But Jackie and Julian, seasoned detectives, never lost

sight of their target. With laser focus, they pushed through the crowd, shouting orders, determined to apprehend Michael at all costs.

In a final, dramatic confrontation, they tackled Michael Cruz to the ground, swiftly handcuffing him as he cursed and struggled beneath their weight. Despite his thrashing and kicking, he couldn't escape the detectives' grasp.

As they lifted him to his feet, Michael glared at his captors, a mix of rage and defeat evident in his eyes. Jackie and Julian stood firm, undeterred. Finally, the justice they had sought was served.

Nancy's heart raced as she watched the scene unfold before her. Michael, her husband of fifteen years, was being restrained by Jackie and Julian, two officers she had tipped off. The gravity of her actions hit her like a punch to the gut.

"What have I done?" she whispered, her voice trembling. As the officers began to lead Michael away, Nancy's guilt and regret exploded into action. She rushed towards them, her face contorted with anguish.

"Jackie, stop! This is all wrong!" Nancy cried out, her voice cracking. Jackie looked at her with confusion, still gripping Michael's left arm tightly.

"Nancy, what are you talking about? This was your idea." Nancy's eyes locked with Michael's. His face, usually so warm and loving, was now a mask of betrayal and disbelief.

"You?" he mouthed silently, the hurt in his eyes piercing Nancy's soul. "I'm sorry, Michael. I'm so sorry," Nancy sobbed, reaching out to touch him. "I was wrong. This is all my fault."

Michael recoiled from her touch, his expression hardening. "Call my attorney," he said coldly, his gaze never leaving Nancy's face. Julian, still holding Michael's right arm, looked between the couple, clearly uncomfortable.

"Ma'am, we need to proceed with the arrest. You can sort this out later." Nancy's remorse quickly turned to anger – at herself, at the situation, at the officers.

"You don't understand!" she shouted at Jackie. "This is a mistake! I was wrong to call you. Let him go!" But Jackie shook her head firmly.

"I'm sorry, Nancy, but that's not how this works. We have to follow through now." As they began to lead Michael away, Nancy's curses filled the air, condemning her own actions and the officers for following through.

Her world was crumbling around her, and she knew that with every step Michael took, their relationship was being torn apart – all because of her misguided decision. The last thing Nancy saw was Michael's back as he was led away, leaving her alone with the harsh reality of what she had done and the uncertain future that lay ahead.

They had achieved it—the criminal mastermind would finally be behind bars, thanks to the unwavering determination of Julian Pratt, Jackie Ortiz, and the Miami Task Force. A swell of pride washed over them, knowing that their hard work and dedication had paid off in the end.

Julian Pratt and Jackie Ortiz exchanged a triumphant glance as they escorted Mike, the notorious criminal mastermind, into the federal detention center. The Miami Task Force's relentless pursuit had finally paid off, and the city's most elusive criminal was in custody.

As they led Michael Cruz through the stark corridors, Jackie couldn't help but feel a surge of pride. Months of sleepless nights, endless paperwork, and dangerous undercover operations had culminated in this moment. She observed Michael's stoic expression, wondering what was going on behind those cold, calculating eyes.

Julian directed Michael to the fingerprinting station, his hand firmly gripping the criminal's shoulder. "Let's get those prints, Michael," he said, unable to keep a hint of satisfaction from his voice. Michael remained silent, his face an emotionless mask.

The fingerprinting process was quick and efficient, but Michael's continued silence began to unnerve the officers.

They had expected gloating, threats, or at least some show of emotion. Instead, they were met with an eerie calm.

In the interrogation room, Julian and Jackie took their seats across from Michael. The fluorescent lights cast harsh shadows, emphasizing the tension in the air. Julian leaned forward, his voice steady. "Alright, Michael. We've got you dead to rights. Why don't you make this easier on yourself and start talking?"

Michael's eyes flickered between the two officers, but his lips remained sealed. Jackie tried a different approach, her tone almost conversational. "You had a good run, Michael. But it's over now. Don't you want to explain how you managed to evade us for so long?"

Still, Michael refused to utter a word. The silence stretched on, becoming almost palpable. Julian's frustration began to show as he slammed his hand on the table. "Come on, Mike! You've got nothing to lose now. Just tell us about your operation!"

Hours passed, and Michael's resolute silence persisted. Julian and Jackie cycled through various interrogation techniques, but nothing could crack the criminal's impenetrable facade. As they left the room, exhausted and perplexed, an unsettling thought crept into their minds: had they truly won, or was this all part of Michael's grand plan? The Miami Task Force had captured their target, but as they watched Mike being led to his cell, they couldn't shake the feeling that this was far from over. The real challenge, it seemed, was only just beginning.

Nancy Cruz contacted Michael's attorney, Lesly Sheridan, a 5'9" Caucasian woman in her fifties. Upon receiving the call, Sheridan promptly donned her black suit, which had been meticulously draped over her office chair. With a sense of urgency, she made her way to the Miami detention center to meet with Michael and ascertain the circumstances surrounding his arrest.

Upon arrival, Sheridan was escorted to a private consultation room where Michael Cruz awaited her. The lights cast harsh shadows across his worried face as she entered. Sheridan wasted no time in addressing the matter at hand.

"Michael, I need you to provide me with a detailed account of the charges against you," she stated, her tone professional and focused.

Michael, visibly distressed, began to explain the situation. "They're charging me with healthcare fraud, Lesly. There are some other charges too, but that's the main one."

Sheridan's brow furrowed as she processed this information. She proceeded to ask a series of pointed questions, seeking to understand the full scope of the allegations and the evidence the prosecution might possess.

As Michael went into more details, Sheridan diligently took notes, her mind already formulating potential defense strategies. The gravity of the situation became increasingly apparent as their conversation progressed.

"Healthcare fraud is a serious accusation, Michael," Sheridan remarked, her voice measured. "We need to approach this methodically and gather all relevant information. I'll need you to recount every detail, no matter how insignificant it may seem."

The consultation continued for several hours, with Sheridan meticulously documenting Michael's account of events. As their meeting drew to a close, she assured him of her commitment to his case.

"I'll begin working on your file immediately," Sheridan stated, gathering her notes. "In the meantime, do not discuss this case with anyone but me. We'll schedule another meeting after your bond hearing to review the formal charges."

As Sheridan departed the detention center, her mind was already racing with the complexities of the case before her. The charges of healthcare fraud presented a significant challenge, one that would require all of her legal expertise and experience to navigate.

Back at her office, Sheridan immediately began researching similar cases and preparing the necessary documentation. She meticulously filled out the paperwork required to represent Michael Cruz, ensuring every detail was accurate and complete.

Meanwhile, news of Michael Cruz's downfall spread through Miami's underworld like wildfire. Gabriel and another highranking member of the Miami syndicate listened as the streets buzzed with whispers and knowing glances, a testament to the adage that bad news travels at the speed of light.

In the world of organized crime, the fall of a titan was always a spectacle. Allies and enemies alike watched with bated breath, waiting for the inevitable moment when the seemingly invincible would crumble. Michael Cruz had been at the pinnacle of power, but as everyone in their circles knew, such positions were inherently vulnerable.

Gabriel, ever the pragmatist, wasted no time in calling a meeting with Raphael. Their primary concern was Michael's wife and kids; Nancy was a loose end that needed to be tied up neatly and quickly. In their line of work, loyalty was a rare commodity, but it existed in pockets, often manifesting in unexpected ways.

During the sit-down, Gabriel laid out his plans with cold efficiency. "We need to ensure Mrs. Cruz is taken care of," he stated, his tone brooking no argument. "Her lifestyle must remain unchanged. The house, the car, all expenses—everything stays as it is."

Raphael nodded in agreement. "Money is no object," he added, understanding the implications of such generosity. It wasn't merely about loyalty to a fallen comrade; it was an investment in silence and continued allegiance.

As they finalized the details of their arrangement, Gabriel was acutely aware of the fragility of their positions. Today, they were the ones extending a safety net. Tomorrow, they might be the ones in need of such consideration.

The next morning, Michael Cruz's lawyer, Lesly Sheridan, arrived at the courthouse early, her briefcase filled with carefully prepared arguments for the bond hearing. She met briefly with her client, reiterating the importance of remaining silent about the case and following her lead during the proceedings.

During the hearing, Michael Cruz's attorney, Lesly Sheridan, presented a compelling case for her client's release on bond, highlighting their ties to the community and lack of prior criminal history. The judge listened attentively, weighing the arguments from both the defense and prosecution.

Judge Robertson responded to Michael's bond plea. He looked directly into Michael's eyes due to the nature of the crime. "Michael Cruz, I should give you a bond, but because of Mr. Cruz's initial actions to flee justice, I will have to deny your bond under these circumstances."

As the hearing concluded, Sheridan scheduled a followup meeting with her client to discuss the formal charges being brought against him and to begin building their defense strategy.

A couple of days later, Lesly Sheridan sat at her desk, her brow furrowed as she sifted through a mountain of documents. Her heart raced as she uncovered one damning piece of evidence after another: financial records, surveillance pictures, and witness statements all pointed to Michael's involvement in a complex web of fraud and embezzlement.

As she dug deeper into the evidence, a sudden ring of her phone startled her, breaking the silence. The caller ID displayed "U.S. Attorney Alice Harper." Lesly's heart raced as she answered, knowing this call could significantly impact Michael's high-profile case.

"Lesly, we need to talk," Alice Harper said, her voice grave.

They agreed to meet at a nearby café. As Lesly walked in, she saw Alice Harper already seated, her face etched with determination. She steeled herself for what was to come.

"I'll cut to the chase," Alice Harper began, leaning forward. "We've got Michael's co-defendants talking. They're testifying before a grand jury as we speak."

Lesly Sheridan's breath caught in her throat. "How many?" she managed to ask.

"Three," Harper replied, her eyes locked on hers. "And they're not just talking to the grand jury. They're prepared to take the stand in open court."

Sheridan's mind raced, imagining the impact of such testimony. She could almost hear the jury's gasps, see their faces contort in shock and disgust.

"What are they saying?" she asked, her voice barely above a whisper.

Alice Harper's expression softened slightly. "Lesly, it's bad. They're painting a picture of Michael as the mastermind behind it all. Every detail, every transaction—they're laying it all at his feet."

Lesly Sheridan felt a surge of emotion—anger at Michael for putting her in this position, fear for his future, and a fierce determination to do her job despite the odds.

"I won't let him go down without a fight," she declared, her voice strong and unwavering.

Harper nodded, respect evident in her eyes. "I wouldn't expect anything less from you, Lesly. But you need to prepare him. This isn't going to be easy."

As they parted ways, Lesly's mind was already formulating strategies, searching for any weakness in the prosecution's case. She knew the battle ahead would be grueling, but the fire in her belly only grew stronger.

Walking back to her office, Lesly Sheridan's passion for justice, for the law, and her duty as Michael's defender burned brighter than ever. No matter how damning the evidence, no matter how many witnesses lined up against him, she would fight with every fiber of her being to ensure Michael Cruz received a fair trial. But little did she know, their conversation was not over.

Lesly received a call from US Attorney Harper the day after their initial discussion. Harper began by asking Lesly's thoughts on their previous conversation, immediately segueing into the main purpose of the call: proposing a plea agreement for Lesly's client, Michael.

The prosecutor suggested that Michael could avoid trial by accepting a plea deal. However, Harper went a step further, hinting at a potentially more favorable arrangement if Michael agreed to testify. Harper referenced the Grand Jury testimony, implying that Michael possessed critical information that could significantly impact the case.

Harper's statement, "he knows what I am talking about," suggested a shared understanding between the prosecutor and Michael about the scope and importance of this potential testimony. This cryptic remark piqued Lesly's interest and raised questions about what Michael might not have disclosed to his attorney.

The US Attorney described the offer as a "sweet deal," emphasizing its attractiveness. This proposition put Lesly in a challenging position, balancing the potential benefits for her client against the ethical considerations of encouraging testimony.

As the call concluded, Lesly was left to contemplate the implications of this offer. She had to consider how to approach Michael with this information, weighing the pros and cons of accepting the deal versus proceeding to trial. The situation raised complex questions about loyalty, justice, and the intricacies of the legal system.

Lesly, Michael Cruz's defense attorney, arrived at the detention center to meet her client, Michael. The sterile visitation room echoed with the weight of their impending discussion.

"Michael," Lesly began, her tone measured and professional, "I've reviewed your case extensively. The prosecution has amassed overwhelming evidence against you."

Michael shifted uncomfortably in his seat, his eyes darting around the room.

Lesly continued, "I believe it's in your best interest to consider a plea deal. The prosecution is offering one, which suggests they want something from you. Is there any information you've withheld from me?"

Michael's jaw clenched. "No," he said firmly. "I want to take this to court. You need to get me out of this."

Lesly leaned forward, her expression grave. "Michael, I must be clear. Your chances of winning at trial are extremely slim. The evidence is substantial."

"I don't care," Michael retorted. "I'm not taking a plea."

"I understand your reluctance," Lesly replied, her voice steady. "However, I urge you to reconsider. The deal currently on the table may be the best outcome we can hope for."

She paused, allowing her words to sink in. "Before our next court date, I need you to think long and hard about this decision.

It's not just about guilt or innocence; it's about minimizing the potential consequences."

Michael remained silent, his face a mask of determination.

"Remember," Lesly concluded, "once we proceed to trial, that deal disappears. The prosecution won't offer it again. This decision will significantly impact your future, Michael. Please, give it serious consideration."

As Lesly gathered her documents, the weight of Michael's decision hung heavily in the air, leaving both attorney and client to contemplate the uncertain path ahead.

Meanwhile, Gabriel, from his remote vantage point, meticulously observed the unfolding situation. Recognizing the need for discretion, he dispatched Raphael to meet with Nancy Cruz. Raphael's mission was twofold: to provide financial support and to gather intelligence on the case's progress.

Gabriel, in his wisdom, understood the immense power of money. While it didn't guarantee silence, it certainly complicated decision-making processes. He reflected on the nature of secrets, acknowledging that true confidentiality existed only when information was confined to a single individual. The moment a second person knew, the secret's integrity was compromised.

In their scheduled weekly conference, Raphael briefed Gabriel on recent developments. He disclosed a critical piece of information: Michael was on the verge of accepting a plea deal. However, Raphael assured Gabriel that Michael's loyalty remained unshakeable. Despite facing legal consequences, Michael steadfastly refused to divulge any information that could implicate others.

Raphael concluded his report with a reassuring statement, emphasizing the enduring bond among their fraternal order: "Not to worry," he affirmed, "brothers for life." This declaration underscored the unwavering solidarity within their organization, even in the face of legal challenges.

As the meeting concluded, Gabriel contemplated the complexities of their situation. He recognized the delicate balance between maintaining secrecy and navigating the legal system, all while preserving the loyalty that bound their brotherhood, the Miami Syndicate (PMC).

Weeks had passed, and the anticipated court date had finally arrived. Leslie found herself in a private meeting with Michael in a secluded backroom of the courthouse. The air was thick with tension, but they were prepared to face whatever the day brought. It was a moment of truth, a culmination of all the preceding weeks' anxieties and preparations.

Leslie paced in the backroom, her heels clicking against the cold tile floor. Michael sat slumped in a chair, his face a mask of stubborn determination.

"Michael, please," Leslie began, her voice tinged with frustration. "I need you to reconsider. Your testimony is crucial."

Michael shook his head firmly. "I've told you before, Leslie.

I'm not testifying. That's final."

Leslie ran her fingers through her hair, exasperated. "I understand you're scared, but"

"No," Michael interrupted. "You don't understand. I

won't do it."

"Michael, listen to me," Leslie said, her tone growing more insistent. "If you want to take this to trial, we will. But I need you to think about what that means."

She knelt beside him, forcing eye contact. "Consider this carefully. For yourself, for your family. Testifying could make this so much easier for everyone involved."

Michael's jaw clenched. "I've made my decision."

Leslie stood, sighing heavily. "Fine. If that's your choice, we'll proceed to trial. But remember, I warned you. This won't be easy."

As she turned to leave, Leslie paused at the door. "Think about it, Michael. There's still time to change your mind and make this easier on yourself."

With those words hanging in the air, Leslie exited, leaving Michael alone with his thoughts and the weight of his decision.

Michael Cruz sat in the holding cell, his mind racing with the weight of his lawyer's recommendation. The cold, hard bench beneath him offered no comfort as he wrestled with the implications of what lay ahead.

His eyes flicked to the clock on the wall. Ten excruciating minutes had passed, each second feeling like an eternity. His breath caught in his throat as the sound of approaching footsteps echoed through the corridor, growing louder with each passing moment.

The courthouse security guards appeared at his cell door, their faces impassive. Michael's stomach churned violently, a wave of nausea threatening to overwhelm him. His hands were cold as they unlocked the cell; the metallic clang of the door vibrated through his bones.

As they escorted him out, Michael's legs felt like lead. Each step forward was a monumental effort; his body screamed at him to turn back, to run, to hide. But there was nowhere to go, no escape from what lay ahead.

Entering the courtroom, Michael's eyes darted around, taking in the familiar faces. His family and friends sat in the gallery, their expressions a mix of concern and support. The sight of them made his throat tighten with emotion.

His gaze then fell upon the detectives, their stern faces a stark reminder of why he was there. What should have been a quick walk to his seat felt like an eternity. Time seemed to slow to a crawl, each step echoing loudly in his ears.

As he finally reached the defense table, Michael gripped its edge, his knuckles turning white. He lowered himself into the chair, the solid wood offering little stability to his trembling body. Across from him, his attorney wore a grim expression, silently reaffirming the gravity of their earlier conversation.

The courtroom's hushed whispers faded into the background as Michael's heart pounded in his ears. The decision before him loomed large, threatening to crush him under its weight. He felt as if he were underwater, struggling to breathe, the pressure of the moment suffocating him.

Michael's mind raced through possible outcomes, each more daunting than the last. The choice his lawyer had presented seemed impossible, yet unavoidable. As the judge entered the room and the bailiff called for all to rise, Michael remained frozen, gripping the table, his future hanging precariously in the balance.

Leslie watched Michael intently, her heart racing as the gravity of the moment settled over them. The courtroom's oppressive silence seemed to amplify every breath, every nervous shuffle.

"Twelve years?" Michael repeated, his voice barely above a whisper. "That's... a lifetime." His eyes, once bright with hope, now dulled with the weight of his impending decision.

Michael's attorney leaned in, his face etched with concern. "I understand it's a lot to take in. But the alternative could be even worse twenty to thirty years if we lose this trial. And the odds are only 50/50 at best."

Leslie's stomach churned as she observed Michael's

internal struggle. His hands trembled slightly as he ran them through his hair, a gesture she'd seen countless times before, but never with such desperation.

The clock on the wall ticked mercilessly, each second bringing them closer to the point of no return. Leslie longed to reach out, to offer some comfort, but she remained rooted in place, paralyzed by the enormity of what was at stake.

Michael's gaze darted between his attorney and Leslie, searching for answers, for reassurance, for anything to make this decision easier. But there was nothing anyone could say to soften the blow of what lay ahead.

As the prosecutor approached, clipboard in hand, Leslie felt a wave of nausea wash over her. This was it. The moment that would define Michael's future and by extension, hers.

Michael took a deep, shaky breath. "I... I need to think," he stammered, his voice cracking under the pressure.

Leslie's heart sank as she realized that even now, at the eleventh hour, Michael was still torn. The uncertainty of it all the possibility of a longer sentence, the risk of trial hung over them like a dark cloud.

Leslie nervously smoothed her skirt as she placed the plea deal documents on the table. Her hands trembled slightly, betraying her concern for her client. "Last chance,

Mike," she said softly, her voice laced with apprehension.

Michael's eyes darted across the papers, his face a mask of growing dread. The weight of his potential future pressed down on him, suffocating and inescapable. Ten years behind bars – the thought made his stomach churn.

"Your co-defendants," Leslie continued, her voice barely above a whisper, "they're turning on you, Michael. They're willing to testify." She swallowed hard, her worry evident in every word. "The prosecution... they have a solid case. I'm afraid this might be our only way to minimize the fallout."

Michael's fingers ghosted over the edge of the documents, his mind racing. The silence in the room grew thick and oppressive. Leslie watched him, her brow furrowed with concern, as the gravity of the situation settled over them both.

"I don't want to pressure you," Leslie added, her voice cracking slightly, "but we're running out of time. The offer expires now we have no more time." She glanced at her watch, her anxiety mounting with each passing second.

Michael leaned back, running his hands through his hair. The enormity of the decision before him was overwhelming. Freedom or a decade lost – there seemed to be no good choice.

Michael's stare fell on the documents spread out before him. The plea deal stared back at him, its terms stark and unforgiving. A decade in prison in exchange for his freedom.

"Some of your co-defendants are willing to testify against you," Michael's attorney continued. "The prosecution has a strong case. This is the best option to minimize the damage."

Michael's jaw tightened as he contemplated the impossible choice. On one hand, the chance to fight and potentially clear his name. On the other, the guarantee of over a decade behind bars. Each outcome filled him with a sense of dread.

After a long, agonizing silence, Michael finally spoke. "Okay. Let's do it." He swallowed hard, steeling himself. "I just want this over with, but I am not turning. I will never testify against my crew."

Michael's attorney gave a sympathetic look, already drafting the paperwork. "I know this isn't easy, Michael. But it's the best way forward."

As Michael's attorney's pen scratched against the documents, he felt a profound sense of loss. Twelve years of his life were about to vanish. It was a heavy price to pay, but one he was willing to accept to avoid an even harsher sentence. With a deep breath, he resigned himself to the deal, hoping against hope that one day he would emerge from this ordeal a free man once more.

Julian and Jackie couldn't contain their excitement as they rushed out of the courthouse, fists pumping in the air. The US Attorney had just announced that they had secured a conviction against Michael, the notorious leader of the Miami Syndicate.

"We did it, Jackie! We took down that slime ball for good!" Julian exclaimed, pulling Jackie into a celebratory hug. Julian looked into Jackie's eyes and whispered, "We got our man. But for me, my next battle is to win your heart. I haven't forgotten our moment in Cancun."

As the US Attorney Harper exited the courtroom, her face etched with concern as she approached Julian and Jackie. The weight of her discovery seemed to hang heavily on her shoulders.

"I'm afraid I have some troubling news," Harper began, her voice low and tense. "Michael's co-defendants have been testifying, and what we're uncovering is... well, it's deeply unsettling."

Julian and Jackie exchanged worried glances as Harper continued, her words painting a picture of a vast criminal network far more extensive than they had imagined.

"The PMC the 'Product Manipulation Crew' it's not just a smalltime operation. What we've uncovered so far is merely the tip of the iceberg," Harper explained, her brow furrowed. "Michael may have been the public face we all recognized, but there's someone else... someone in the shadows pulling all the strings."

Jackie's hand trembled as she grasped Julian's arm. "What are you saying, exactly?" she asked, her voice barely above a whisper.

Harper glanced around nervously before leaning in closer. "We believe there's a mastermind behind it all. Someone who's managed to stay completely off our radar until now. And the worst part? The PMC is still out there, still active, still wielding significant influence."

Julian's face paled. "But I thought with Michael's arrest..."

"We all did," Harper interrupted, shaking her head. "But this goes deeper than we ever imagined. "The PMC the 'Product Manipulation Crew' it's not just a smalltime operation. What we've uncovered so far is merely the tip of the iceberg,"

Harper explained, her brow furrowed. "Michael may have been the face we all recognized, but there's someone else... someone in the shadows pulling all the strings." Michaels's Co-defendant and the debrief they talk about. Someone that Michael would talk to on a clone cellular phone to make a final decision. He would always make that phone call. Michael never used his name, always an alias. Calling him his brother, he would often refer to him as a playboy because of his lifestyle, living good, money, women, and power.

As the gravity of the situation sank in, a cold dread settled over the group. The battle they thought they'd won was far from over, and the enemy they faced was more powerful and elusive than they'd ever anticipated.

Harper's phone buzzed, breaking the tense silence. "I have to go," she said, her eyes reflecting a mix of determination and fear. "But please, be careful. We don't know how far this network extends or who might be involved."

As Harper hurried away, Julian and Jackie stood frozen, the worried atmosphere around them thickening with each passing moment. The victory they'd celebrated now felt hollow, overshadowed by the looming threat of an unseen adversary still at large.

Meanwhile, Gabriel Cortez and Raphael Santos sat together, enjoying Cuban cigars and celebrating with a bottle of bourbon.

They raised their glasses in a toast to Raphael's leadership role in the Miami Syndicate and their shared future.